FIC   Lette, Kathy, 1958-
        Girl's night out

$16.45

DATE			

OCT   1989

Girls' Night Out

By the same author

Puberty Blues

Hit & Ms

Girls' Night Out

Kathy Lette

William Morrow and Company, Inc.
New York

Fic

Library of Congress Cataloging-in-Publication Data

Lette, Kathy, 1958–
Girls' night out/Kathy Lette.
p.   cm.
ISBN 0-688-08511-3
I. Title.
PR9619.3.L447G57   1989
823—dc19   88-35691
CIP

Printed in the United States of America

First U.S. Edition

1 2 3 4 5 6 7 8 9 10

BOOK DESIGN BY PATRICE FODERO

FOR KIM

*And thanks to all my mates—especially Al,
Cara, Liz, Jen, Pen, Ang, Catho, the Killer
Koala, my Mum, H.B., Humph, Alison, the
seaweed munchers, the footy heads, the Hair Bear
Bunch, and Penny for her ripper editing.*

Contents

He's Coming at Seven

He's coming at seven. He promised. Handle it. Act normal. It's your personality he's hot for, you tell yourself as you pumice toes, steam blackheads, razor pits, apply lip bleach and an organic face pack consisting of cucumber, honey, yoghurt, and egg whites. "One must feed one's complexion, Deb," Julia reckons.

6:00 P.M. Your face is starting to ferment. You stand anchored in the middle of the room. *Ferment . . . !* The grog! Julia said that red wine needs untold time to breathe. Gouging out the corky residue, you tell yourself to get your act together. *Breathe?* What is it? Asthmatic? Whack it near the vaporiser.

Take a squizz at the label. My God! What if he can tell you bought it on special, that this "cheeky little Hunter Valley Red" cost only $4.99 including complimentary packet of pretzels? Remember how he told you in the lift at work about his photographic palate, how he can distinguish the area, the year, the grape, the soil . . . *probably the picker's name.* "Most men, Debbie," Julia had raved over brekky, "think women have no wine palate." You grab your sloppy Joe and high-power it to the corner pub. It is only when you try to ask for a nice, dry white and can't move your mouth that you remember you're wearing the face pack. The egg whites have set like cement. Worse than an egg head, you're a human omelette.

Trying not to smudge your "Malibu Passion" nail polish, you let the Frog vino slip from your hands to its death on the dirty pavement. Half your bloody weekly salary. You try to squeegee it back into the bottle with a hanky.

6:30 P.M. Oh well, if the food's perf, he won't notice the plonk. After all, it *is* the way to a man's heart . . . although that isn't exactly the part of his anatomy in which you're interested. "It'll close up, mate, if you don't *do* something. And *soon.*" It takes Kerrie a long time to come to the point. But it's all right for her, she's got a whole smorgasbord selection of classic spunkrats. It'll be beaut to finally have a bloke to brag about at the Girls' Night Out.

Give cooking the flick. Instead, you go and squeeze Ortho-Gynol over your diaphragm. It's tongue-numbing, you know, but once he's got that far, there won't be enough time to conduct a sneaky safari for his vasso scar. "Insertion should be a part of foreplay," Kerrie had crapped on that morning through her Special K. So your diaphragm is left waiting on the bedside table under its foaming white doona of spermicide.

After an arm-wrestle with the garlic crusher over the guacamole, you pig out on a bulk bowl of beans. Ergh! Heavily into the gorge, you recall Kerrie's warning—not to eat anything which will cause intestinal distress. "Fill up on water, Deb. Then he won't see you for the gutsy, farty, greedy pig you really are." You vow to eat yoghurt till your tongue starts to curdle. If only you were one of those glam girls in restaurants who pick at lettuce leaves and look as though their *minds are on more important things* . . .

With your bottom thrust towards the mirror, you crane over your shoulder. Puke! Ergh! Not only have you got a two-tone tan from lying on your board all day, but you're the ultimate Human Bowling Ball. . . . But if your behind is a problem, what about your *mind?!* Justin's an A-grade journo. You'll need scuba gear just to talk to the guy. *Talk?!* Talk. What about? At Julia's dinner party the other night, all the guests sat round reeling off work deals, latest theatrical projects, economic theories. The most interesting thing that had happened to you all week was getting your ears pierced. Your head swivels over the other shoulder and there you are again, gawping into the mirror. Why? *Why* were you born with a big bum and a low brow? You knicked off from school when you were sixteen, four years ago, so you're not so much an eminent as an imminent intellectual. He is an Arts graduate with a degree in journalism. The only Shakespearean quotes *you* know are off a desk calendar. You have a Ph.D. in desk calendars. Writhe into these control panties and size-eight jeans. Justin is an Intellectual. *He knows the difference between Iraq and Iran.* You have now cut off the circulation to both denimed legs. Your last boyfriend, a conehead computer freak, broke it off 'cause he reckoned you were an illiterate waxhead. Frantic, you begin rehearsing spontaneous dialogue. The Nicaraguan situation? The storage safeguards of nuclear waste? Pressurized fluorocarbons? . . . Handle it. Who cares what boys think. It's cool anyway. You're not illiterate. Your olds were married when they had you.

6:45 P.M. Hide your surfboard, wet suits, and dope plants under the bed. Don't want him thinking you're a Bong Brain. You notice the houseplants have more or less carked it. Julia reckons you should talk to your pot plants. . . . *Shit!* nearly seven o'clock. Tell your plants just to talk amongst themselves.

7:00 P.M. Why bother cultivating houseplants anyway?

11

There's untold alien vegetation sprouting, untended, behind the toilet. You ricochet around the flat, hiding and tidying. Scoop out the dead goldfish with a tea strainer and flush them to a disinfected grave down the dunny. Plan to make off-the-cuff quips about your domesticity being limited to brewing trouble and sewing wild oats.

7:05 P.M. You notice there are two toothbrushes in your cup. Some male wombat from long ago left this grungy, chewed-up dental memento. God! He will think you have *Another.* Or *Others!* Then he'll wonder what *they* have. Like *herpes.* Hide it in the bottom of the bin.

7:06 P.M. Put cellophane on the overhead fluorescent. Sip your second gin and tonic. Sigh. Yes, things are looking much more romantic.

Disease . . . *You're* not deadset diseased. But what about *him?!* How to bring it up subtly? Julia warned you that all blokes should be examined carefully before attempting anything carnal. Breaking away from a passionate embrace and spreading his legs with a ten-battery power torch would sort of dampen the romantic ambience somewhat. You unwrap the overhead fluorescent and collapse back into the beanbag.

Deep breaths. Stay calm. Ommm . . . Ommm . . . Ommm. Think of clean, clear surfaces. Empty spaces. Nothingness. *Nothingness!* Your eyes trigger open. Gaze at your flat as if for the first time. What does it say about you? It says clean, clear surfaces. Empty spaces. Nothingness. Why can't ambience and charisma come in a spray can?

7:30 P.M. Go for it. You grab an armful of Julia's books and scatter them about. Some poetry in the loo to convey sensitivity. Some psychology by the phone to suggest depth. On the coffee table, some learned tomes to hint at the unusual, in fact, the full-on uniqueness of the Real You. (If you'd bothered to examine the titles you'd have seen they read *Taxidermy Your Budgie* and *What Your Navel Says About You.*)

Not that you want him to think you are a pure full-on intellect. A head-and-a-half man like him would only appreciate a woman with a love of aesthetics. Jesus bloody Christ . . . You rummage through Julia's end of the record collection. He is coming at seven. He promised. If you're quick, he'll arrive to find you casually listening to Gluck's Twenty-first Symphony for triangle and Renaissance toenail harp.

8:00 P.M. Mr. Punctuality-plus . . . Must've been held up at the newspaper. *Yes!* He'd complained in the canteen that some office chick had got the files out of order. Don't be a dag. Control the impulse to call. You slurp your G and T and casually flick through a coffee book on Angora goat pasturing. Slam it shut. What the fuck do you know about *goats?* A glance around the room renders you panic-stricken. What if what you see as compellingly eccentric, he sees as full-on certifiable? Catapult around the flat collecting all the planted books. Drill yourself in Meaningless Drivel: who's up who at work, genetic differences—practise rolling the sides of your tongue inwards.

8:30 P.M. It *is* fashionable to be late.

9:00 P.M. Not *that* fucking fashionable. How long does it take to flick through a pile of files? An organised filing cabinet just means you lose things alphabetically. You leap up from the chair. Jesus! You don't want to be just vegging out when he arrives. He mustn't be allowed to think that you don't have bulk other things to do. Or bulk other people to do them with. You rush back into the bathroom and retrieve the shaggy toothbrush from the bin. Justin's a real rager with a big by-line. He would like his women wild. Mull up. Rub some dirt back onto the toilet tiles. Dishevel the bed.

Kerrie warned you that the first time in bed with a new bloke is always a bummer. Well, how premature could ejaculation be? He wasn't even here yet. . . . There's a smell of something burning. Under the hot bedside lamp your diaphragm has melted and blistered into a pale rubber poppadom.

10:00 P.M. You sag, as though you are part of the beanbag and contain nothing more than little polystyrene baubles. What's so hot about being an intellectual anyway? It sucks. You're pissed off with dinner-party dialogue you need an encyclopaedia and dictionary to decipher. Since Julia scored you the journo's job as surf reporter and you moved into Darlinghurst, your conversation's been limited to full-on vocal genuflection. "Deadset?" "Amazing!" "Incredible!" But, you address the ice cubes in your glass, fuel formulas for Exocet missiles and the names of toxic molecules located in tubercular calves' lungs do not come naturally.

The answer is suddenly obvious. Julia's friends swat for dinner parties. They feed themselves thesauruses intravenously. "The jeremiad has definite iconographic, epistemological, and solipsistic innuendos." Intellectualising—you turn to lecture the guacamole—is about saying more and meaning less. Wrench off your jeans. In size eight you can either look trendy or breathe. You can't do both. Justin's the yobbo. Not you. Contorting out of your control panties, you decide to quit dieting and just have one of those operations to cut the excess arse off. You know, a labottomy.

10:30 P.M. You placate your misery with the bowl of guacamole, all the while assuring yourself that those pretzel-thin chicks in restaurants have no food for thought. They're too superweary from lack of fibre to lift up a fork.

11:00 P.M. Rehearse some new conversation topics: suicide statistics for single women; radical celibacy; lesbianism. Put on a Tammy Wynette Country and Western song about being unloved and all alone. Using your hairbrush as a microphone, you mime into the mirror. "He hasn't even rung," you croon as another chorus to the song. And the goldfish didn't even flush. There they are floating forlornly in the toilet bowl.

11:30 P.M. There is a certain irony to it all, you tell your tenth gin and tonic. A wrought irony, you tell your eleventh. An overwrought irony, you address the carpet where your body has found accidental sanctuary.

The hands of the clock hinge on midnight. He was coming at seven. He promised.

Dial his home number. Don't be naïve. Prepare yourself for the voice of Another Woman. A man answers. Idiot. It *is* the eighties. Behind every successful man is the Other Man. Ask for him.

"Yes? Justin speaking."

At the sound of his sleepy voice you start to giggle. "There's, there's only one thing . . ." you're crying now, "you need to know about Iran . . ." Pause to burp. "It's going from Iraq to ruin."

Free Kick

ook love you won't last the season. I've seen groupies
come and go. I've bin with footballers twelve years. And
I'm the only one they talk to at the club. Youse young
groupies are idiots. Youse get drunk and whinge, "Oh,
you're talkin' to another girl." Na. You won't last the season.
There are rules, see. Like not being obvious. Like when you
go to the club, you don't walk up to a footballer and start
chattin'. It could be embarrassin' for him. Like wiv Leanne
and me, that's Leanne-Leanne-the-Footy-Fan, we walk into
the club and we stand at the bar. If they wanna speak to us,
or they wanna arrange a night, or whatever, they've gotta
approach us. We don't go and chat to them. That's rule
number one. Neva ring their home, neither. Most of 'em
have silent numbers and that, anyways. And um, keep
your mouf shut. You don't talk about who you've bin in bed
wiv. Or what you've done. Smoke? Hang on. I'll get us an
ashtray.

And you don't screw round. See I know my boys are all
faithful to me. 'Cause all the blokes I bed and that in the

17

team are happily married. They've all got about six children. And most of our footballers are policemen, see, in real life, so their reputations are on the line. They've gotta be careful. So, if you're gunna mix wiv my footballers, you can't sort of screw any Tom, Dick, and Harry, and then go and sleep wiv my team 'cause that puts them at risk. 'Cause if they picked up an infection or AIDS or somethin' and gave it to their wives, all hell would break loose, see, and the club cops it. The wives tend to be very abusive and they blame the clubs 'cause their husbands are screwin' round. Or the poor bloody coach. That's why when I seen you down at Woolies I grabbed ya for this little chat. 'Cause if *you* stuff up, we all suffer. It was a year ago the last young one, and well she gave the jack to about free or four of 'em. That's right and all those warts and things they got. All the wives told their husbands that they weren't allowed to go to the pub after trainin' and if they did they were gone for half an hour only. Like Gibbo. When he goes to the club, his wife gives him two dollars to go out wiv. So the guys gave this young groupie type of a person the flick. That's why the older guys just mix with me and Leanne-Leanne-Footy-Fan. No. You won't last the season.

But . . . seein' as we are Stick Sisters, like, right at the moment . . . What? Ya dunno what I'm on about? Well, like it started at school. When ya found out you was bein' two-timed, you'd get together wiv the chick he was sharin' his stick wiv, and send the guy a twig. . . . You did do business like wiv the whole team didn'tcha? Yeah, well, if you're gunna do it, you may as well do it right. There's a um, you know, like an etiquette in the sack, see. They like a good gobble first. And then usually they're in a hurry 'cause they've gotta rush home to their wives, so they just jump on and do their little deed. But you've gotta feed their ego. It's good for their confidence on the field and that. They like to

18

think they're doin' you a favour. Like Jacko. Jackson's like
. . . well, he's all right in bed. He's not brilliant. You know,
when he blows he pretends he hasn't. Like he'll sort of put
his dick in and he'll have a screw for a minute and . . . he
always likes the other blokes to watch, see. And he goes first,
'cause he's captain. And so he says, "Look at me go!" And
he goes an' then after about a minute, he'll blow, but he'll
just sort of keep goin' . . . "Right, now I'll have your legs up
over me shoulder." He's already come, but he sort of exhib-
its himself for another fifteen minutes after he's done the
deed. And you've got to go, "Oh, oh Jacko," you know, and
carry on. It wouldn't be good for team morale if the blokes
knew their captain was a dud bash type of a fing. Right? And
the team comes first.

I've got a bit of bubbly. Excuse the mess and everythin'.
It's too wet to hang the washin' an' that up outside. Fancy
a drink? It's a bit flat but . . .

Nuthin' will get you the flick faster than fallin' in love.
You've gotta say to yourself, he's got a good body and I use
his body like he uses mine, or it just won't work out. Like,
you get groupies who hang round and they fall in love and
they bug 'em and Leanne an' me stand back and you can
see they say, "Ah you fuckin' moll" when the girl walks
off, or they say, "Oh here she comes again!" and they hide
behind the poker machines. These guys are under enough
pressure from trainin' and that—we've lost the grand final
four years runnin'—they don't need any extra worries from
you, right?

Andja gotta know your football. But don't mouf off like
Wendy the Wog. She's revoltin'. She's a grub. And she
doesn't tub. And she says, "Oh you did this wrong and you
did that wrong." Like, the coach knows what went wrong
and he'll sort it out wiv the players. Coaches don't need
bloody mad supporters with red and green or blue and yel-

low brains stormin' at the blokes the minute they walk into the club after losin' a match. They also hate groupies that hang round sayin', "Oh you were superb today . . . brilliant," when she most probly neva even went to the game and the bloke spent the match on the bench.

I hope you appreciate, well, like it's a privilege to be selected as one of their groupies, even if it is just for a season. My first graders are heroes round here. They're the most respected guys in this whole area. And you've gotta live up to the, you know, honour-type fing. I like a bit of competition. I like a chase. Like, they're fairly hard to get onto some of the first graders. Like, the older footballers are more sort of "Oh, me wife's here. Don't sort of speak to me" type of attitude. And a bit hard to get. And I like that. Like, when I was about sixteen, I had this crush on Prong. He was the hottest footy player on the field. Everyone was creamin' their jeans over him. He was famous for this long prong of his. Anyway, my brother was playin' snooker up at the Catholic Club one day; it was lunchtime and he'd told a few of the fellas that I had the hots for Prong. So the next fing I know, I'm gettin' paged to the foyer. So off I toddled and answered the phone and this husky voice on the other end says, "Meet me down near the butcher's. Down the bottom of the club." So I um, walked downstairs and so Prong's standin' there and he says, "Come on, we're goin' to this bloke's place."

So um, we went to this guy's place and he took his clothes off. And I'm looking at this twelve inches of his. And I said, "You're not gunna put that in me." And he says, "Oh yes I am." And then afterwards, he explained all about team spirit and that. "Get your end in, get your friend in."

So, that's the way they do it. Tag team. It helps 'em play together better. Except the coach. When he comes in the bedroom, the uvver guys are s'posed to leave and shut the door. It's a sign of respect, see. 'Cept the younger guys, they don't always obey the rule. Standards have really dropped since the younger blokes started gettin' into first grade. Trouble with the younger ones, the ones who brung you up the club, well, no offence love, but they're a bit too easy. No standards.

Like, the older footballers, they show a girl more respect. When I fell pregnant, this is when I was barrackin' for Prong's team at the time, all the guys brung me round flowers and chocolates in hospital and that. I know Prong denied she was his. Even though, like, Tiffany's the spittin' image of him. It wasn't his fault but. I'd never fallen pregnant. I didn't realise . . . Like, when I was fourteen, I got raped by about firteen guys and I was torn inside and um, the doctor told me I'd neva get pregnant. I neva expected to fall pregnant, so I neva took the pill. So in that situation I can't blame him for farvering a child. . . . Smoke?

See, I got drugged in a hotel when I was a virgin. Me girlfriend was fifteen. And me uvver girlfriend was sixteen. And they were the biggest molls that walked the face of the earth. Slippery and Wok-eye, have you heard of 'em? We were down at Burwood. I was in The Royal Sheaf. So um, I was up there and I got drunk and someone had slipped a mickey in me drink. And um, I'd only had a few. . . . Like, I wasn't a one-can wonder. I used to drink beer at home wiv Dad before he choofed off, and I'd only had about two sips of this beer and I was frowin' up and delirious. See, they was jealous 'cause I was a virgin. I don't fink the guys they set me up wiv realised that I was a virgin. And um, this guy said, I'm gunna take you for a drive to sober you up. 'Cause that was before I got expelled from school, so I had to go home to me muvver's—I got expelled for callin' the nun a lesbian. The blokes just fought I was a slut like Slippery and Wok. But I was probly the only girl in the whole school who didn't go to bed wiv blokes and that. See, I was too embarrassed to take me clothes off. 'Cause I didn't have any titties or any pubies. Yeah, me girlfriend, she said she had this girlfriend that didn't have any pubic hairs and all the guys she went to bed wiv called her "Tennis ball." So I said to meself, "Oh that's not gunna be me. I'm gunna grow some parts before I go to bed wiv a bloke." Have you got enough room? Put all them toys on the floor. We was lucky to get this flat. Lotta unmarried mums live in this block and we sort of look after each uvver's kids. There's just these coupla rooms and the kitchen. It's kinda cosy but.

And anyway, um, he drove me down National Park and I was delirious. Everythin' was just all blurry. And all these guys were pullin' themselves on me. All I remember is sayin', "Don't. It hurts. It hurts. It hurts." And about a year later I found out that the two girls had set me up wiv all these guys. But they got their own. Like they're heroin addicts and prostitutes now. One just had a baby in the women's prison. And one got busted for heroin and got both her children taken off of her. So in the long run, they got what was comin' to 'em. What about some Cheezels? They're a little bit soggy but, sorry.

Anyway, one night I got drunk and rang up Prong's muvver and said, "Would you like to see your granddaughter?" And she said, "Oh, I'll have a word to my son about it." And Prong just denied that she was his. Like, he didn't deny it to me. He come round a few nights later and got rool aggro. It's not his fault. They need a certain amount of adrenaline, footballers, to get out on the field, see. He gave me a hidin'. Roolly bashed me up badly. But see, I'm pretty soft-hearted. I wanted to charge him with assault and then drop the charges. Which is what I did. I got told by this senior sergeant to do that, to put a bitta wind up him, so he knows that he can't get away wiv it. I mean, his

22

farver's a millionaire. They, like own this big bridge construction company type of fing, and um, he's left the force now and he's like co-owner wiv his dad. I mean, I didn't wanna be greedy, but he coulda paid just a little bit of maintenance. . . . But then, he was um, they used to call him Bryan Brown, he was a rool glamour boy, like the rugged, handsome type, you know? And he was the favourite at the police station. So of course when some little "hussy" decided to charge the favourite cop at the police station with assault, you know, all hell broke loose. A few of the detectives got a bit dirty on me. Leanne reckons that was why me flat got raided and I got busted for dope and that. But I was the sort of team mascot. Na. It was a coincidence. The coppers I knew neva woulda set me up like that.

So, anyway, Leanne-Leanne-Footy-Fan and me, we was only rool young, and we got blind one night after a big match and we started givin' the blokes marks out of ten. I gave Prong a score of two. And Reggo nine. Jacko was round the next day tryin' to break the record. Anyway, the blokes who got the low scores made sure we got the flick pass. So it was our own faults. But strewth it was funny.

So, anyways, we moved out of that area and I've bin wiv this team ever since. I was only seventeen then, like you. That was eleven years back. You're okay, you know that, kid? Wish I had some photies of 'em. See, in my travels—I used to move round a rool lot—I dunno, I just lost everythin' on the way. But look, I cut some snaps of Prong and Spud an' the boys out of the newspaper. I keep 'em in the cupboard where I keep the spices an' that. No one'd neva look in there. See? Hot hunks huh? Don't you dob me in neither. If the uvver boys ever saw I had piccies of anuvver team, I'd get the flick pass. I still fink of 'em sometimes. . . . More bubbly? Especially when I look at Tiffany, I see Steve, that's his rool name, see.

Tiffany and Alexis, the way I'm bringin' them up, is to be street-smart. Not like their muvver. Like, a couple of weeks back some of the guys were round here and there was this new guy, the new little winger we've got, and the guys were intimidatin' him. They was sayin', "Oh, look at it," you know. "Look how little it is," and flashin' their well-hung bits. And I said, "Go outside so I can concentrate on this new piece of meat." He was that nervous. And um, they said, "No. The kids are out there." Alexis and Tiffany were out there watchin' TV and I said, "That's no excuse," 'cause they've known Tiffany, that's me eldest one, like, you know, since she's bin born. And so Tiffany must have bin hearin' me sayin', "Get out of the room. Give me ten minutes," 'cause she knocked on the door and said, "Wouldja like me to make youse all a cup of coffee?" She's ten. Very well mannered. Very feminine. Very bright. She knows what goes on. She's got, not a hatred towards men, but she understands what women go frew wiv men. Like, I just want my little girls to be more street-smart than me. Like Alexis the uvver day. The soft-drink man come round and Alexis is too young to really understand, she's four . . . oh well, she does, but she's funny. . . . The drink man, he knocked on the door and Alexis said, "Go into the bedroom and take your clothes off. The condoms are in the cupboard." I cracked up. She's funny though, isn't she? Sweet little treasure. Give Mummy a kiss. . . . Her dad's a detective. You know Grub? Speakin' of drinks, a top up?

Actually, none of the guys have bin round this week. Not that I live for them or anyfing. I don't, like, you know, depend on them or anyfing. But, I mean, sure, it does get a bit lonely here at home. 'Cause, I mean, I've got two children. I can't go out. Except to the shops and to the game. So, I mean, the footballers liven fings up, you know. Like, the uvver week, I was sittin' at home watchin' the wrestlin', when there's this knock on the door. Grub, that's Alexis's farver, he's the, you know, detective, arrived wiv about seven blokes on a bucks' party. I had a girl stayin' here called Cheryl. She's called Slippery Dip, do you know her? 'Cause of her tits. A rool big girl. She's an ex-prostitute. She hasn't worked for about five years as a pro but she's a horny little fing. And apparently she was roolly good in bed. She did all these fings that I've neva even done. When she was havin' oral sex wiv a man, she'd take him, take his penis, all the way down her froat and just sort of move her froat type of fing and he'd ejaculate and I fought she'd choke but she didn't and the blokes was ravin' about her after the bucks' party. And I was sayin' to her, "What didja do? What didja do?" You know, I fought she'd taken me spot wiv the team type of fing! And nobody's neva gunna do that, right?

Anyway, see, oh they were funny. The wrestlin' was on, and they you know, all these guys, I'm sort of sittin' there and all these big policemen—most were from the team, and the uvvers play on the police side—were climbin' up on the back of the lounge and they were jumpin' and landin' on their shoulders, doin' wrestlin' you know, and jumpin' and gettin' each uvver in headlocks. And someone had this video camera type of a fing, and they were makin' porno movies. Only there was no film in the camera or nuthin'. But Slippery Dip fought there was, so she's lickin' her own tits and that, like this . . . How's your glass? What about some dip? Here we go. French onion.

Grub sort of grabbed me and I said, "Oh yeah," and we went straight to the bedroom. So, like I'm givin' Grub a suck and he's on the bed and this uvver guy, Marto, well he's creeped up from behind me, underneaf me legs and got his head on the back of the bed and he starts lickin' me out. Footballers neva lick women out 'cause they think women are, you know, internal. I can understand it in a way. Most of 'em are good in bed but. I haven't roolly come across too many duds. I blow real easy but. Anyway, you can imagine, I was that shocked. It was real cosy. Just the free of us. And Grub, he freaked out. He says, "Why aren't you concentratin', Tracey?" and I said, "Oh God, how can I concentrate?" you know, and he said, "Is Marto lickin' you out, is he? That bastard." Grub gets real jealous. Especially if I mix wiv any of the lower grades. I think, you know, he hasn't admitted it to himself type of fing, but he's roolly in love wiv me. 'Cept he's always been a confirmed bachelor and that. . . . So it was a top night all round. Sure beat watchin' the wrestlin' with Cheryl. On our, you know, lonesomes. Alexis! Get out of the dunny. There's germs in there, petal pie.

Anyway, so I was up the Leagues on the Sunday and this Cheryl chick well, she's roolly moody, you know, and she's big, about five foot eleven, and she turned round in the pub and in front of everybody she says, "Oh, look at the old slut over there. She gets porno movies taken of her at her place." Me muvver goes to the local church see and the barmaid up the Leagues is a rool strict Catholic. And she goes to church wiv my muvver and she's looked at me. And I just fought, "Oh, you bitch." And all these people who know, you know, me rellos were in the club. "They took porno movies of her at Grub's bucks' party." That's what Cheryl said. That it was Grub's bucks' party. And she sort of laughed.

So anyway, I charged at this girl and I nearly killed her. There were four footballers hidin' under a table. 'Cause I frew chairs at her and bashed her and I really laid her out. Oh, she can fight, but I was cranky. And about five blokes had to drag me off of her. But these old blokes, they were like sort of, you know the two old guys in the "Muppets" that sit up in the balcony? They were like that. They sat there sayin', "Me money's on the little red-haired one." All the guys had bets on me. And they're goin' round collectin' money. She was pullin' me hair. And I was pullin' hers. And she says, "Let go of me hair. You're hurtin' me. If I let go of yours, will you let go of mine?" And I said, "Er no, I like it." Then I held on to her head and punched her in the face.

It wasn't her lyin' about Grub havin' a bucks' party or the porno stuff, or the fact that me rellos were all in the pub, or the fact that she's such a grot—she's given poor Murph gonorrhoea twice and once she got crabs off Splodge and gave them to everybody—but, see, I had to stick up for the footballers 'cause she was droppin' names. She was sayin' I'd had porno movies done with Jacko and Marto and Grub. You know? And I had to bash her, 'cause of their reputations. I don't worry about mine. I neva regret what I do and I don't have to, um, answer to nobody, so I do whatever I want. But they've got a reputation to lose and a family and wives and that, so I was more or less stickin' up for them. Besides, I've known Grub for off and on, oh, seven years. Wouldn'tcha reckon he'd have told me if he was gettin' hitched? Wouldn'tcha?

Anyway, last Saturdee was Alexis's fourf birfday party. Grub was s'posed to come. But he never fronted. And I rung him at home and his best mate said, "Oh, he's gone to pick up his tuxedo, he gets married today." And like, the woman he married had free children to him that I didn't even know about. . . . The tide's gone out. . . . Top up?

So I, um, got drunk and gate-crashed the wedding reception and fronted up to him. Like, I wasn't upset for myself, understand. I couldn't give a stuff. But for Alexis. Like that's a rool horrible fing to get married on her birfday. And the coach was there. Like I'm an Aries and well, this stupid dickhead of a coach, he's new and just doesn't like me. This coach just started draggin' me out of the reception place for no reason. He's a rool idiot and Grub turned round and laughed right at the wrong moment. Like I'm gettin' dragged out of the place and he turns round with a big smile on his face and I just turned round and clocked him. Bloody oath I hit him. Broke his nose. I give him the best hit you've ever seen. Wiv one punch I fractured his nose and split all his mouth open. See, I, like had free bruvvers and they used to bash me. So I think it's sort of, you know, kind of survival. I just shape-up, like a bloke. Then I got dragged out of the club and Grub's farver got up to hit me. And I frew the red telephone in the hall at the coach 'cept it missed and ended up hittin' this rool heavy detective. There were lots of "D's" there.

It wasn't that he was gettin' married. Like I said, I couldn't give a stuff. It's just that it was Alexis's birfday. And I was a bit blind. And I'm Aries. And I was feelin' rool emotional 'cause we'd lost the first match of the season. To the Parras. And I reckon it was Grub's fault. He'd played rool lazy on the field. He'd let the whole team down, you know. He'd only bin thinkin' of himself. He didn't even take into account the hopes and that uvver people might have had pinned on him, right? For the match and that I mean . . . How's your glass? What about some Brandivino? It's left over from the party.

You wanna know the secret to my success? Why I've lasted eleven seasons? I don't act like a wife. I mean, I don't mean that rudely because wives . . . I've neva bin a wife, I don't know how they act. But from what I've heard, they get moody and, well, I s'pose that's normal, but um, they nag, from what I've heard, they nag their husbands—where have you been, what have you done? That's why they need us . . . need me, right? If I'd wanted to be a wife, I coulda had any of the guys. They'd stand in line to wed me, right. I just neva want to be a wife, right, neva.

It's just that Grub always showed me a lot of respect and that. He owns like a deep-sea cruiser, and when he's rostered off he takes tourists and that out on the harbour. And every time he comes round here he always brings the leftover prawns and potato salad, you know, left over from the cruise and that.

See, my boys really need me. It's like a marriage, but to the whole team. Like I've got all their addresses and phone numbers and that . . . I've got somebody who checks up for me at the Motor Registry and I get their dates of birf and I send them birfday cards an' that. They always freak out. Oh, I send them to their work addresses but. It's just they don't want me wastin' me money buyin' cards and that, see?

You'd never get consideration like that from the younger players. Oh no, the younger guys in the first grade have got sort of different attitudes. All they want to do is make money. They're highly competitive professionals too, which means they don't get up the pub as much and have fun. But when they do, they get rool arrogant and act like idiots and call you a slut and carry on, even though they've neva even bin there to call you one.

It was just that Grub was different to the uvvers. He'd like do fings on the spur of the moment. Like he'd come round . . . we'd make love anywhere. Rootin' on rocks in parks, in the freezin' cold. Out on the cliffs. One time, he and his mate come round and um bipped the horn about eight o'clock in the mornin'. "Come on. We're goin' to the club." I left the kids with Nola, she's my neighbour on this side, and I run downstairs, get into the car and they took me into the storeroom at the Leagues Club. Grub's a copper see, and he's got keys to everywhere. They'd just finished sort of early-morning trainin'. So they was all clean and showered and that. Usually the guys get ya to lie back on the big bags of potatoes. It's roolly cold in the pantry and the sacks are rool lumpy. But Grub, he's taken off his jacket and put it on the ground for me and said, you know, "Lay down on this." Footballers don't usually offer their jackets to get all messed up. You know. Usually blokes say, "Ergh, don'tcha put your spermicide on me jacket. The wife might smell it or somethin'." Not that I was in love or nuthin', right. But Grub was different to the uvvers. It was sort of gallant for someone to lay his jacket down. It was just so . . . romantic.

I belong to that team, see. That new coach, he just can't ban me from the club for life. I've even got the team name tattooed on me privates. And on me hip too, with a heart and a scroll. They'd be lost without me. I mean, I don't look too bad do I? I'm not an old boiler yet. Am I? There's no way they'd dump me . . . is there?

That's where you'll screw up, see. You're young, see. You haven't toughened up. You'll do somefing dumb like fall in love, see. Look love, you won't last the season.

Vegetable Magnetism

1/1/83—Day One on the Road to Enlightenment, Inner Peace, and Harmony

Sitting on my haversack outside McDonald's with Cat.

When I told my mother that I was suffering from the oppression of Western conditioning, she thought I was talking about shampoo. With parents like that, is it any wonder that I'm spiritually malnourished? Why can't they be separated, or in mid-life crisis, or discovering an Eastern religion like everybody else's parents?

Read my mum's palm and explained that this was a fingerprint of her potential. All she wanted to know was whether or not she should go ahead and book her P & O cruise. "But Ro, is it there, in my destiny?" she kept saying. Let me tell you, they'll be sorry when they're reincarnated as a couple of cockroaches. (Oh God, a Valiant load of unenlightened yobs are pulling into the curb. I'll lay a heavy trip on them and pretend I need a lift to a Women Only Trance Workshop.) The only thing my family gets a buzz out of are germs. Philippa, my big sister, puts her hand over her plate every time I pass the tomato sauce or marg or anything, in case a bit of Cat's bacteria does a Kamikaze leap off my clothes onto her chop. I tried to influence their eating habits. Really, I did. I threw out the Sara Lee cakes and Corn Flakes. But you should have seen Philippa the morning her muesli was moving. Okay, there *were* a few weevils, but they would have been organic for God's sake. I bought it at the Health Food Shop. There was no need to chunder all over the breakfast table.

How can anyone ever attain Spiritual Enlightenment living in a family like mine? Let alone develop a third eye. My family has a third-eye infection. (A 120 kmh rich bitch just wagged her 18-carat finger at me disapprovingly.) My olds keep telling me it's a stage I'm going through. I hate it when grown-ups dump that on you. It's totally *age-ist*. Discriminating against someone for their age is just as prejudiced as race discrimination. Think my parents have gone senile. (A hotted-up Holden just screeched to a halt down the road. Enlightenment, here I come!)

I'm back. As I lugged Cat and my haversack over to the car, gravel flew, tyres squealed, and the bunch of thugs drove off hooting their horn and screaming with laughter. It's such a drag to have to deal with people who haven't been introduced to the nonstructural, free-flowing, wing chun-gung-fu of their inner consciousness. It's because I don't want to be a member of the yobbo-teriat, like them, that I set out on my path to Spiritual Enlightenment, Inner Peace, and Harmony and answered an ad in the Health Food Shop to take part in a low-impact, nonsexist, antimaterialist, personal-growth orientated, cosmic consciousness-raising commune. (Month's rent in advance. Credit cards accepted.) Have to go. Have a feeling I'm going to get a lift in this coal truck.

Think I'm clairvoyant. (I knew I was going to write that!) The truck driver has asked me to stop scribbling and talk to him about something riveting, or he'll fall asleep. He *is* looking very red round the eyes and keeps sneezing. Probably eats meat. Will tell him about my family.

Have just had a close call with destiny. Within two sentences, he fell asleep and was swerving off the road. That's how riveting my family is.

1/2/83

What with alter egos, ids, past lives, rising star signs, and schizo personalities, there are about twenty-five people living on the commune. Everyone is mohair and very organic. You could plant seeds on them.

"Ro, we do not believe in ego, aggression, negativity, jealousy, or ambition," Sundram asserted. He must be the tribal elder. He looks at least twenty-eight!

"Me neither!" I agreed to hurl all those emotions onto the compost heap. Then this circle of bodies in batiks and lap laps enveloped me. Zultana asked my star sign. There was no way I was going to confess to being a jealous Scorpio with a rising, egotistical Leo. (Couldn't my mother get anything right? She could've held on a week or two for the sake of my personality.) Told them Aquarius. It's not really fibbing. I just changed my astrological sign by Star Poll.

I was then instructed to share my inhibitions with the group. (My earrings had already been shared—they stripped my overloaded lobes minutes after my arrival.) I looked at them blankly. "Um . . ." Up until now I didn't think I had any.

Camille readjusted the batik notted round her pelvis. "You're inhibited about being inhibited." She's been crowned Soya Bean Queen for two years running. She is too beautiful to be true. I keep glancing down for a stapled navel or a *Playboy* page number.

"You've gotta get into, you know, your inner soap opera, Ro." Sky has three kids, pierced nipples and nose, and her legs are festering as her body expels city toxins. Shows how little I know. I thought they were tropical ulcers.

Spent the rest of the afternoon getting into some Core Contact, Colonic Cleansing, and a Past-Life Odyssey Workshop. Sundram was once a Roman emperor, Camille, a Chinese princess. My cat turned out to have many past soul mates and to be on a higher plane of crystal awareness than any of us. They renamed her Kublai Khat. I couldn't come up with anything. Even if I *do,* it'll probably be a bank clerk.

Oh well. Have so much to unravel and learn about myself! Had no idea I was so incredibly fascinating!

P.S. In a few weeks I should be able to have my first ever primal scream!

1/6/83

The sun is glaring down like a 100-watt globe and the wind is as hot as a hair drier stuck on triple speed. Paterson's curse and lantana cover the paddocks all around us. Everybody else is meditating.

The truth is, my meditation is not so much transcendental as accidental. You know, a numb state that overtakes me in bank or loo queues. Camille doesn't seem to have any trouble slipping her brain into neutral. It's not fair! Why can't I be a vegetable like her? I know the way to Spiritual Enlightenment is through inner consciousness, but how can I concentrate on emptying my mind, when emptying my mind is on my mind?

1/7/83

Sundram is the *most* enlightened, spiritually advanced, and uninhibited person on the commune—he farts openly.

1/14/83

I think Sundram feels romantically inclined towards me. He keeps following me into the communal dunnies. The first time he said hello, I nearly fell in. Obviously I am the *least* enlightened, spiritually advanced, and uninhibited person on the commune. But I find it very hard to reciprocate romantically when squatting over a ten-foot septic abyss. Sundram advised me just to go with the flow.

1/25/83

At first I reckoned the lack of food in the fridge was 'cause some cheapskate scabs were not putting into the kitty. But it's just that the hippy trippers up here are heavily into spiritual nourishment. Like this afternoon, Sundram was drying a tray of marijuana in the oven. "Din-dins," he said, scooping up a rustling handful. "Why live real life . . ." he dragged in the smoke with relish, ". . . when you can vegetate?" When the chillum died, he took it from my hand and peered into my upturned palm. "Okay babe . . ." With his lungs full of smoke, his speech was strained, as if talking over a burp. "You . . . Ro . . ." he exhaled, "are ruled by your head and not by your heart. What you gotta do, is stop being hung up on middle-class, puritanical bullshit. You gotta relax, liberate, free yourself up." Sundram placed my diagnosed hand firmly on his penis. "Sex is a form of meditation. Our sex energies could meet and really merge, you know? Have you ever heard of the Cosmic Orgasm?"

Sundram explained to me that he has to have sex, otherwise his chances of getting cancer of the prostate are increased. Poor, poor Sundram! Oh well, Cosmic Orgasm here I come!

1/26/83

Sundram's double mattress is on the floor, a mandala and mozzie net suspended above it. A huge pile of marijuana is stacked in one corner. He's going to sell it in Sydney. Not that he's into money. But just to buy some essentials (compact disc, car, and Float to Relax tank). Sundram says that consumer goods are cleansed of any superficial materialism when used for the purpose of psychic enrichment. This means I can now save up for an Akai video.

Sundram wears these really cool seventies batiks. Seeing me gasp for breath once he'd disrobed, he explained that the pressurised fluorocarbons of deodorants destroy the ozone layer. I really admire his stance but must take care to keep my nose out of his armpit. Naked, his body is encrusted in tight black curls. He reminds me of one of Mum's Steelo soap pads. I stretched out on the grey flannel sheets so we could get down to scouring.

"Send a message to your uterus, not to, you know, conceive," he said afterwards. "It's *your* body. Concentrate. *Will* the sperm to leave your system."

"We didn't kiss . . ."

He looked at me incredulously. "There are more germs in the mouth than in any other part of the body." So, while he's curled his back towards me and sunk into a stoned sleep, I'm there issuing orders to my ovaries!

2/2/83

I think Sundram is, like, incredible. He agrees. I now know without a doubt that I am in DEEP spiritual love—I let him cash my dole cheque.

2/3/83

A week's gone by and still no Cosmic Orgasm. This could be because I am busy emitting positive vibes to the carpet snake coiled around the roof rafters of Sundram's room while simultaneously trying to tune into the frequency of my ovaries.

Unlike me, Camille is really in tune with her body! Every day she drinks a glass of goat's milk with a pill made from cow placenta. She spun out tonight about the burden of being beautiful, how it obscured her personality and aura. Poor Camille! Sundram got her head back together with some passive joint manipulation. He says with help she can change. Sundram reckons anyone who doesn't believe in miracles is just not a realist.

2/4/83

Declined Sky's kind offer of a massage. Don't feel remotely tense.

2/5/83

Sky keeps heavying me about the dangers of tension buildup from the repression of bad karma.

2/6/83

Have begun to feel tense about not feeling tense.

2/7/83

"It's Camille." Sky was straddling my back and her kneading intensified. "She's, like, really you know, fake. She just won't get her sexuality act together. She uses her body in this really sexist-type way." My wad of shoulder muscle was being wrung like a Wettex. "I really feel much more like kind of now . . . than I did then," she said profoundly. "Ya know?"

I told Sky that Camille was just generous. "Yeah," Sky agreed. "She's given most of the men on the commune a dose of one disease or another." I raved on about how hard it must have been growing up with mega-rich oldies. Her parents gave Camille this farm, just to make her feel guilty about it. As if all that's not a heavy enough number, she also suffers from premenstrual tension. Poor Camille! She's been premenstrual for months! But she really is trying to channel her psychic energies. Camille has asked Sundram to help her exorcise her bad childhood experiences using a rebirthing technique. This is where you lie in the bathtub naked and go back to the actual moment of your birth. You can see the doctor's face and everything!

2/14/83

Wish I could meditate. Apparently the urge to sink into a deep transcendental trance can strike you at any given moment. Though I've noticed it's usually when there's washing up to be done. You know, if I weren't into being an Aquarian, it would really give me the shits that Tarzana and Zultana and the others are always talking about workers uniting, but they never wash up. Not once.

Sundram, on the other hand, is really disappointed that he can never help me make dinner. "From my years of communal living, I've developed an acute awareness of the exploitation of women. But unfortunately I don't have time for domestic duties. I'm studying for next month's Men's Consciousness-Raising Seminar. Sorry," he corrected, "Ovular." (The word *seminar*, Sundram feels, does not encourage a cycle of ideas.)

2/27/83

Camille is making real progress with rebirthing. She has realised that her headaches are the result of her having been a forceps delivery. What's more, the reason she gets stuck in relationships is because she was in the birth canal for ten hours. (Boy, am I glad I was a Caesarian.)

2/28/83

It's amazing isn't it that you have to get a licence to own a dog in the suburbs, but that any yob can have a baby. Wish more mothers were like Sky. She believes her children are on a higher plane of awareness. She got Lennon from a truckie who gave her a lift to Noosa. And Zero (she doesn't want him to have an ego) is from a really real relationship she had with an astrologer yoga teacher. Camille reckons she got Moon Unit from an Intuitive Preceptor Heart Master, Dr. Love Ananda. She selected all the fathers by their looks. At first I thought it sounded a bit weird. But well, you've heard of Calvin Kleins. . . . So what's wrong with slipping into a bit of Designer Genealogy?

3/1/83

Am a bit worried about whether or not my ovaries are coming in-over-and-out. Asked Camille about contraception. She said she uses the rhythm method.

3/28/83

You know what they call a woman who uses the rhythm method? Mother. Camille is pregnant. She has obviously lost contact with her Fallopian tubes.

3/29/83

Camille threw the I Ching to see whether she should abort. (Sky's abortion method is to insert seaweed and drink malley root juice.) I think the father's an unenlightened yob for not being supportive. Sundram, thoughtful as ever, is helping her make the decision by contacting her inner self.

3/30/83

Camille's mother must have had a very traumatic labour. Sundram and Camille have been locked in the bathroom reliving it for hours. Her poor Mum could've had triplets by now. Strange groans and gutteral whimpers are filtering out underneath the door.

About time I learnt not to be so selfish. Will start by getting my healing act together and helping Sundram with Camille's rebirthing in the bathroom.

4/1/83

Sundram is interested in Camille's inner self, all right. All the way in.

4/2/83

Had my first flash of a past life! I was an Egyptian princess. The Gods demanded a human sacrifice and I had to choose between my slaves, Camille and Sundram. I chose Camille.

4/3/83

Sundram says that sex is just a bodily function. I suggested that in that case, they could just have a bowel movement together.

Sky said that I behaved in a possessive, jealous, and unenlightened manner (all I did was dump a bag of fructose mash and bean curd over Camille's head) and that I should simply sleep with someone else.

4/4/83

Today I had my second flash: Sky's children are going to grow up to be vacuum-cleaner salespersons.

Too late I realise the spiritual depth and devotion of my union with Sundram! The only reason his dope pile has dwindled is because he's so generous to the spiritually poverty-stricken. I mean, he couldn't have smoked it all on his own. Anyone who could consume that amount of cannabis would be a total social reject, a Bong Brain addict, wouldn't he? He's asked for my dole cheque again and I'll gladly give it to him. . . . I know I can never, ever be attracted to any other man's sexual yang!

4/5/83

Today I intercepted a letter for Sundram from the dole office and found out that his real name is Simon Crudd. And hold on to your asteroids—he used to be a merchant banker. That explains why he is always talking about investing in people, psychic income, and balancing energy levels. That also explains why he uncaps the mineral water to let it breathe for at least two hours before drinking.

Now I know why I never had a Cosmic Orgasm.

His yang has gone sort of yuk.

4/10/83

Camille said that Sundram read her palm and told her she was ruled by her head and not by her heart and that sex is a form of meditation and that their sex energies could meet and really merge, you know, and they'd have a Cosmic Orgasm and that saying no was increasing his chance of getting cancer of the prostate. . . . "Besides," she said, "right now I'm just trying to get my relationships clear, whether they're straight, or gay, or both. I'm not clear on who I really want, Sundram or . . . you."

Well, *I'm* not sure I want to get involved with someone who consumes dehydrated cow placenta every day. You'd never be certain you wouldn't find her outside grazing on the kikuyu.

5/2/83

Am now sleeping with Ulysses. It's okay. He kisses.

5/10/83

Got caught eating a bit of chocolate. "You're not supposed to eat chocolate, Ro, because of the chemicals," Sundram reprimanded. "Okay," I said, "I'll just eat the chocolate bits and spit out the chemicals."

Sundram got really angry then and shouted at me that we should only eat vegetables, because vegetables keep us passive and good-natured. He has vegies on the brain. Not grey but green matter. He also said that if I was going to eat chocolate I should've shared it. That's what a commune is all about—sharing. (Yeah, boyfriends included!) Camille just gushed that it was a "high-fibre snackoid situation" and started to chop food for the wok. Sundram confiscated the miso he bought in town. Sky had a fit because someone drank past the high-tide mark she'd pencilled on her bottle of goat's milk.

The fridge is full of paper bags marked with people's names and fruit-juice containers branded "poison" to deter thirsty strangers. Sky is snapping at Camille to stop dicing the bean curd. "That bean curd's mine, shitface." There we go, sharing and caring again . . .

5/16/83

Nobody is speaking to anybody else. Sky says we're going to have an encounter group and "unblock the shit in our emotions." It's the first time I knew I had an S-bend for a psyche.

5/18/83

Having decided our parents are to blame for everything we all feel much better. Ulysses was actually kicked out of home! Not just 'cause of his dope bust and tropical ulcers, but his unenlightened parents couldn't handle his body-detoxification programme!

5/20/83

Looked up body detoxification in the *Your Body Yourself* book. It involves drinking a glass of your urine first thing every morning. Reliving all our early-morning kisses, I finally felt a primal scream coming on and chundered all over the breakfast table.

5/23/83

Vegie patch needs weeding, sheets need washing, roof needs mending, sink needs unplugging, carpet snake needs catching, and the cops need placating about the commune's overdue parking fines. Nobody around to help. All gone astral-travelling.

5/25/83

Don't know why everyone's so keen to find intelligent life on other planets, when it hasn't been found here on earth yet.

5/30/83

Been thinking it over, and well, maybe this isn't the decade for Vegetable Magnetism. It's the eighties, right? The environment's full of chemical crap, right? Yin and Yang is about balance and harmony, right? As much as we might dislike it, we've got *no* choice but to pig out on hamburgers, veg out in front of the telly, and get drunk on Girls' Nights Out and crap . . . that way we'll balance with all the crap in the environment. Right?

5/31/83—Day 151 on the Path to Enlightenment, Inner Peace, and Harmony

Derailed.

6/1/83

Think I'll be a punk.

Police Bulletin: Positive sighting of Missing Person, Rowena Taylor. Seen hitchhiking towards Sydney.

REPORT

Illegal Alien: Simon Crudd, operating under the alias Sundram. Believed to be an illegal astral-travelling alien. Wanted on charges of growing marijuana.

Misplaced Person: Sky. Lost—one identity. Believed to have left her brains at the Queensland border.

Deceased: Ulysses. Blood poisoning.

Mistaken Identity: Camille last seen in the company of a Reincarnation Guru. She now operates under the alias of Empress.

Located: Rowena Taylor. Inner city. Wanted on driving offences, for running over dogmas with her karma.

CASE CLOSED

The Sushi Sisters

The Cockroach Belt

All the men were ugly. Underarm odour, bites, blisters, in-grained grime, and soiled "Life Be in It" underpants. They all leered up at me from the massage table. "Any extras?"

This parlour was my first job ever, after fleeing the sub-urbs that morning. My mother's pursuit down the driveway was as hot as the rollers in her hair. I'd threatened to run away zillions of times, but it was year ten that finally pushed me into packing my swag. The day before I'd asked my maths teacher to explain why it would benefit me in later life to know how to calculate the gradient of a railway line as it rounded a bend. "Silence, when speaking to a teacher," he'd said. In kindergarten they spend all their time teaching you to talk. In high school they spend all their time teaching you to shut up.

At Central railway station, I'd lassooed the ad for "Chiropractor's Assistant" in black felt pen and walked to Newtown.

You know how you feel when you're crook in the guts? Well, this guy *looked* like nausea *feels.* The badge on his white coat, which he immediately shed, read "Ron Smart. Chiropractor." He sprawled starkers on the slab and instructed me in kneading techniques. When he flipped sunny-side up, his erection practically sprang into my eye. Wondering whether to go under, over, or circumnavigate it, I administered a vocal cold flannel by delivering an enthusiastic lecture on the gradients of railway lines. He told me how much to charge per massage and what my percentage would be. I'd scored the job.

He'd hired one other masseuse, a punk-looking girl called Mouche. About ten earrings dangled from each pendulous lobe. She wore striped socks, coloured gym boots, and an op-shop tangerine-colored organdie ball gown. It was the sort of dress you have to be poured into. And nobody had said "when." A couple of years older than me, she was *terribly* suave. Through the Ryvita-thin partition separating the two cubicles came a low wolf whistle. "What do you want me to do, mate?" I heard Mouche snarl in reply to her lecherous customer. "Bark? Or just piss on your leg?"

I'd finished my customer first and was flicking through a prehistoric copy of *Cleo* magazine in the grotty waiting-room. In between the ads for Modess and freckle-removal creams was a story about Roxanne, who had hungry thighs and walked on the wild side of New York night life devouring men. I had just got to this really tacky part where Roxanne had entered Plato's Retreat, a bar where you check in not your coat but *all your clothes,* and was deciding whether to go into the Group Grope or the Lezzo Rooms, when Mouche emerged from her cubicle.

"Finished?" Her fingers, like mine, were blackened with dead skin.

"Na. I've just left the creep in there with the box of Kleenex."

"He's *not?*"

"He *is,*" she said casually. I watched her slip off the casing of a lipstick and tattoo the floral wallpaper. "Men suck," she wrote. "I wanna get the sack s'arvo." Mouche told me that the CES were suspicious that she never attempted to find work. This stint would shut them up for a bit, she said. "Say . . . it . . . with flowers . . ." I dangled on every Hawaiian-Sunset Max Factor letter. "Send . . . your . . . man . . . a triffid . . ." Mouche was what you'd call street-smart. I, on the other hand, was Middle-of-the-Road.

My next customer lurched up onto one elbow. "What size bra cup, love? I'm a photographer. Professional. Get orders for everyfink. Big rumps, little tits, amputees . . . Some guys just wanna come and watch the modelling sessions frew a peephole." Urging him to lie down, I attempted to give Mouche some SOS semaphore through the porthole in our partition. "If guys can get their kicks jerking off over a photo or two, saves birds like youse from being raped, right? One of the little girlie's who's working for me— started two months ago—now she's hit the big time. Got her own Ford Laser, a flat, and everyfink." He sized me up. "B cup . . ."

Hearing the outer door wheeze open, I extricated myself from his conversational Gladwrap. Two massive men in suits swelled into the waiting-room. My fingers ached at the sight of their mounds of muscle. I looked at Mouche. She was scrutinising the tips of her bleached hair for split ends then peeling apart the delinquent strands. My vile customer appeared in his birthday suit at the cubicle door.

"Detectives," Mouche hissed at him. It was like vocal Mortein. He withered and was repelled out of sight down the street and away. They were looking for our boss, Ron

Smart. "Well, he obviously *wasn't,*" Mouche snorted, retrieving our day's earnings from the desk. "He's not a roolio troolio chiropractor, is that it?"

"Warrant for arrest,"—the detective's delivery was like a pneumatic drill—"on a murder charge." They asked for our names.

I prepared to give a dossier of dates, hobbies, favourite colours, vital statistics, political preferences . . . "Joanne Prit . . ."

"Tracey Wonderley," Mouche interjected. "And Karen James." (It was news to me.)

"How old are you?" the other D asked me.

"She's seventeen," Mouche lied with ease, "and I'm eighteen."

He proceeded to lecture me about the importance of self-respect and how easy it was for girls to be led from the path of virtue. I nodded. I nodded at everything he said, like one of those dogs who sit in the back windows of cars in the western suburbs. "Well, Tracey," he addressed me, "you should just thank the Lord it's not you sprawled out on a meat tray down in the city freezer."

I did. I thanked Him, then and there. And we weren't even on speaking terms. See, I come from a spiritually schizo family. My mother's a Tyke. And my Dad's a Prot. Every night my Mum would tuck me in and we'd do our "Hail Mary Mother of God" prayers. "Go to Catholic scripture class tomorrow, darling, won't you?" Next, my Dad would come to my room and we'd go through our flip-side religious repertoire. "Gentle Jesus meek and mild . . . Church of England scripture class tomorrow. I'm counting on you . . ." Caught between the poles of my devout parents, I grew up an ardent believer in atheism.

The monotony of his moralistic voice set my smiling head nodding on its spring once more. Mouche was shovelling everything portable into her Mary Poppins bag—clock radio, tissues, towels, and a year's supply of baby oil. While the detectives ransacked the premises, she yanked me out the back by the elbow. "Come on . . . *Tracey.* " She hurled her bag, discus-style, over the paling fence and shinnied up after it. Shell-shocked, and with the theme music of *Miami Vice* blaring in my head, I rushed after her. We thudded down into the back lane. "Never give a cop your name, dickhead." She looked at me for the first time—at my Sportsgirl spotted dress, filed nails, and pink clip-on earrings. "And change your clothes. You look like a suburban wanker getting round in that clobber. Hoo roo!"

I was having enough trouble coordinating my speech, let alone my clothing. I trailed her up the lane way. She cast disparaging glances over her shoulder, then stopped, whipped a small wad of notes out from under the elastic of her underpants, and swivelled towards me.

"Here y'are. In times of panic," she peeled off half the notes and thrust them at me, "keep cool and collect. That'll get you safely back to the Lamington Belt."

"I'm not going home."

"What! You've pissed off?"

"I wanna be a singer. Or a dancer. Or a poet. Or a novelist . . ."

"Which one?"

"Dunno . . . Whichever comes first."

"Great," she said with a crooked grin, sizing me up. "Go for it. Nobody else in this shitty country gets off their arse to do anything, so if you do something, you'll *make it.* "

The city-bound bus lumbered into view. I flicked through my address book. It had about two people in it. The family dentist and my relief English teacher, Imogen. Nobody wanted to teach in the western suburbs. We'd had relief teachers to relieve the relief teachers who were relieving the relief teachers. Everybody else would have liquid-papered me out of their address books by now, especially the rellos. The bus belched blue exhaust.

"Didja know in New York there are nightclubs—my words did somersaults to get over the top of each other— "where you don't just check in your coat, *but all your clothes!*"

"No shit?" she laughed. "Do you know how to catch a bus?" I looked at her as though she was a yobbo retard. "Giggle a lot," she shouted above the roar of the diesel, "blush a bit, look down lots, stand pigeon-toed, forget where you're going for a minute, chuck him a cheesy, and then ask for half-fare. Got it?" And she yanked me on board.

Steaming hot water pummelled my back. I scrounged a flimsy piece of disintegrating soap from the holder. It was encrusted with pubic hair. Plump women, their skin deeply flushed, scrubbed away at dimpled thighs and cellulite. One scrutinised a mole under her left breast. Another blew her nose into her fingers and flicked the snot down the drain between her feet. Girls with India-rubber breasts arched lithe bodies and razored fresh crops of pubic stubble.

Mouche had blackmailed a university student into giving her his sports-union badge. Every second day she came down to the sports centre for an illegal shower or a swim in the chlorinated phlegm.

I'd been nurtured in cotton-wool wadding. It hadn't prepared me for Mouche. She was exotic. Not only did she live in a squat, write songs, wear no underchunders, carry a switchblade, and dye her pubes the same colours as her hair ("collars and muffs" she called it), but she could also execute fanny fats. "It's just a burp," she explained, "backwards." She played a tune then and there. New Blue Clinic foam frothed in disgust all around us. "I could teach you. What tune do you want to learn?"

I thought for a moment. " 'Auld Lang Syne.' "

She laughed. "May old acquaintance be forgot?"

"And fast."

"Anyone in particular?"

"Just men in general. After this morning, I've gone off them."

"What?" She doused me with cupped handfuls of water. "As a genre?"

But the best thing about her was her laugh. It was a tropical noise that warmed everyone around her. Mouche could do anything: pierce earlobes with an ice cube and needle, tell the size of a man's penis by the length of his index finger, play guitar and piano, and sing. In the showers she started to make up a song about men "eating up their ladies . . . a perfumed lunch . . ."

"In the back of the Mercedes," I added, and she wove it into her melody. We ad-libbed lines, groping for rhymes, letting the tune gel, and then harmonising. By the end of three verses and a chorus we had dead men's fingers.

"Where you gunna crash?" I didn't exactly have a string of Hiltons offering me poolside penthouses. Before I could answer, she nudged me, indicating the girl in thongs flapping her way across the tinea-infested tiles. Mouche chucked her a cheesy. "Excuse me, but like a complete moron I forgot my shampoo. Do ya reckon I could borrow just a smidgen?" Mouche returned with a small, green pool of chemicals in the palm of her hand and frothed my hair into a luxurious lather. "You can crash at my place." She scrutinised me. "You're a bit straight for it though."

"I'm not! I've done *everything*. Gone with guys, smoked dope, sniffed glue, shoplifted, sung up on a stage, been to Bali . . ."

"*Shit!*" she snorted. "You're world bloody weary." She gave me a hairy eyeball. "I like you." There was a sudden acidic smell of urine. All the showering women glared at each other accusingly, toes curling back from the communal drain. "You make me laugh."

In the toilet cubicle, I camouflaged the seat in layers of dunny paper. In all my fifteen and three quarter years, my mother had only imparted a few pieces of wisdom. Never end a sentence in a preposition, never take the Lord's name in vain, always press lift buttons with your knuckles and turn off taps with your elbows, and *never* sit on a public toilet seat. Not wanting to contract any trendy venereal fauna, I kangarooed it. Poised there in a crippled leapfrog, I craned to decipher the graffiti on the top of the door. "Why bother to squat?" it mocked. "Germs jump ten feet." I got the feeling that, unlike Roxanne, I would only have checked in my coat at Plato's Retreat. When it came to walking on the wild side, I still preferred to tiptoe.

The squat was in Woolloomooloo. Plaster dandruff hung in flakes from the ceiling. The walls shed their striped felt and pastel pastoral scenes. They all needed a rubdown with Vaseline Intensive Care to prevent peeling. During redecorating binges, furniture too heavy to shift had obviously been painted over and round. In the absence of tenants, the squat now displayed fuchsia-pink and lime-green interspersed with large slabs of purple. Reproductions of works of art were nailed, glued, or smeared over all the walls. From the concave roof dangled an amputated chair leg. Dodging it, I then bumped my head on a stolen street sign. TURN BACK, it read. YOU ARE GOING THE WRONG WAY.

"Welcome," Mouche said, "to the heart of the cockroach belt." Max emerged from the debris. Anorectic and cultivating a very healthy crop of acne, he was more pretzel than person. "This is Jo. I thought she could help us with the rent."

His eyes, encrusted with mascara, puckered with a sort of glee. "Absolutely. And the phone and hot-water bills and interest rates and loan repayments and electricity . . ." he smirked. I was yet to see how we did survive without all these things. "The pipes sweat like they need an antiperspirant. And you can only put loo paper down the dunny after lunch."

"Max is going to put a sign out the front," laughed Mouche.

"Out of Order. Use squat next door."

I liked him instantly. Max didn't dance on thin ice, he did his callisthenics there, in Doc Martin boots. Drug-rehabilitated and on a good-behavior bond, he had just been released from his parents' protective custody. He appeared with a plate of melted Kraft cheese on toast. There was a thud from upstairs.

"Mong," Max informed us through the strands of cheese. "He's been there all arvo."

Mouche paused. Her mouth, then her whole face, contorted.

"Mong?"

"Lloyd. The love of her life," Max explained. "We call him Mongoloid. Hence the Mong."

"We had this bizarre night. In Paris . . . not the *town.*" She responded to the surprised twitching of my eyebrows. "The Paris *Pub.* In the dunnies. I was a bit off my face and he came into the Ladies' after me and we locked ourselves in a cubicle and drank more piss and then all I can remember is my bum in the air, pink tiles, the toilet bowl, and lying on my back. And then when we came out, I chucked a glass of wine at him, and then I fronted up to this band rehearsal one day, and he was there and I hadn't shaved my legs, and he said, 'Love ya hairy legs' and I thought, 'fucking creep' and he asked me if I wanted to reenact that night at the Paris and I told him I didn't root short men and soon after that he moved in."

"Gee, how romantic." It made my friendship rings and gropes at the drive-in (the Finger Bowl as it was known locally) look like one of Keats's love poems. I heard Mouche hand Mong his emotional-eviction notice.

"You was only usin' me. Youse feminists are fucked. For me body and that," he spat.

She agreed and hurled his baritone ukulele and home-made bong down the stairs after him. "I loathe wimpy men," she explained to me.

So he was out. And I, apparently, was in.

Mouche's room consisted of a disembowelled mattress and a tarnished mirror. Tights and strangled T-shirts spread in a spaghetti entanglement of coloured cotton around the perimeter of the room. The back bedroom had been sort of scalped, the roof removed for repairs and just never re-placed. The only place to sleep was in Mouche's bed, with Mouche.

I didn't know why she had brought me home. I had caught her eye, like a dress in a window. She had got a crush on my cut-and-colour combo. Nothing Gucci mind you. I was your very basic drip-dry nylon. But I think she liked me most 'cause I let her squeeze my blackheads. She loved to do that. I would lie with my head in her lap, holding a torch over my face, and we'd talk.

"Would you eat me? . . . Hold still, wouldja? If our plane crashed in the jungle?"

You could have great convos with her. All the shallow shit you'd be too embarrassed to talk about mostly. Comparing navels, innies or outies. Deciding whether or not you'd give in under torture. And what would make you snap—knives, cockroaches, spiders, or being locked in a room full of real estate salesmen.

"Ouch! Not so hard!" I squealed. "All they'd have to do is threaten to send me back to my parents, and I'd tell them everything!"

"Couldn't threaten me with that. Thank God. Must be nothing worse than having to bring up your oldies." Mouche had told me in the showers that she was the by-product of foster parents and youth hostels.

"Well, what *would* make you break?" I peered up into her face. Her acid-green eyes had more than a glint of larrikinism. Mouche wiped the residue of a whitehead on the leg of her jeans. Her fingers read the bumps in my face as if they were braille. "No more orgasms."

That first night we talked till our faces fell off. Finally, we wormed underneath the malnourished blanket. The room was like a stage-set beneath the neurotic glare of a streetlight. The night noises of sirens and cat shrieks were new and scary. For as long as I could remember, I'd fallen asleep to the whirr of the dishwasher and the sound of my parents' slippers working their way through the superdeluxe shagpile. The more I tried not to think about my parents, the more I thought about them. They had always had really high hopes for me, you know, that I'd become a kindergarten teacher or a chemist's assistant. Ever since I'd announced my "artistic vocation," my dad and I had only been on grunting terms. He would come home every arvo from the air-conditioning plant, grunt, then go out the back to water the above-ground Clark pool. He was always watering the pool. I guess he hoped it would grow into an Olympic. Mum pretended to handle the announcement of my chosen career. Yet for the last few weeks, instead of detergent, she'd been regularly pouring guinea-pig pellets into the washing machine, so that all our clothes emerged a slime-grime green.

I replayed their reel-to-reel rhetoric. "You'll come running home pregnant and in trouble with the police"; "By the time *you* find yourself," my father would quip, "there'll be nobody home."

With the low-tide mark in my bank book, after another week I'd be stuck on the monetary mud flats. I gazed at

Mouche's profile on the pillow. She had extraordinary looks. Beautiful. A strong face, dark features, not the kind of beauty for advertising tampons. Her hair was a spiked, coiffured creation that could have been used as the base of a flower arrangement. And the bitch had no blackheads. I had found a friend. I curled up against her naked back for warmth, and cupped together like two spoons, we fell asleep.

The next day Mouche took me up to register at the dole office. "They're bound to offer you something shitty," she said and proceeded to coach me in ways not to get the job. 1) Wear daggy, filthy clothes; 2) Always arrive late; 3) Put "buts" on the end of every sentence and speak with rising inflections; 4) For "previous profession," write poet, harpsicordist, and/or platypus desexer (part-time); 5) When asked if you have any questions about the job, say yes, just one: When are your holidays?; 6) Swear. A real fucking lot.

The clerk flicked through a file of pink cards. "Skills?" Her manner suggested that I'd failed nose-picking classes in kindy.

Skills? Well, I could hit top C, get picked up hitchhiking by a man with an erection and not get raped, cook cheese-on-toast, skindive for abalone, rhyme difficult words. I was an apprentice fanny farter, with an okay vocabulary (except I spelt finetically. Inphuriating, huh?), and had a very finely tuned crap antenna. It wobbled most violently in the presence of brownnosers, school prefects, racists, real estate blokes, married men, and—she tapped her lacquered talons on the tabletop. "Ah . . . none," I confessed—*and* supercilious CES clerks—"Age?" . . . who suffered from ageism. "Fifteen and three quarters."

She dealt me out a destiny. I read the card between her tailored nails. A chicken-gutter trainee in Zetland. "Begin today." Mouche had dressed me in a moth-eaten, glittering mini-skirt ensemble. The clerk peered at my flesh through the sequined portholes. "Don't bother trying any tricks. They take all the dregs."

Men are always saying they can count the number of times they've cried on the fingers of one hand. Well, I reckon women can count the number of times they've really done their blocks. Most women, that is. Not Mouche, "Who do you think you are?" she spat, snatching the card, "God?"

The clerk buzzed her next client, eyeing us coldly. "Yes."

"Yeah, well, we're atheist." Mouche shredded the job card and stomped from the office, swearing. I followed her down Oxford Street.

"Don't they, you know, kick you off the dole, if you don't take the job they offer . . . no matter how daggy?"

"Those wankers expect us to be grateful for that kind of shit. Newspapers are always whingeing about the dole bludgers. Shit it's the *dividend bludgers* that are fucking the country."

I fingered the few dollar coins I had in my pocket. "Mouche, I know being on the dole is like being on an insulin drip, but at least it sort of, you know . . . *sustains life.*"

"Chicken gutting in a factory is just a slow form of suicide." She detoured through the post office, slamming the coin-return buttons on the row of red phones. The last one discharged a twenty-cent piece. "Why kill time, when you can kill yourself?" She pressed the coin into my palm. "We'll survive," she smiled. And then and there we made a pact never to surrender to bedpan emptying or bank-teller jobs.

And so our adventures began. We busked on street corners and snow-dropped clothes from the backyard Hills Hoists of trendy Paddington. (They say charity begins at home . . . just select your neighborhood carefully.) For food we ate leftovers. It was a case of putting our mouths where our money was. Paddy's Market fruit vendors gave us their cast-offs. But you had to eat them fast; they were just this side of mould. Still, we needed those daily doses of penicillin to keep the bacteria at bay.

Merchandise hurled itself off the backs of trucks in Woolloomooloo. And Max was always there to catch it. One week we lived on canned lentils, the next on muesli slices, while we wondered how to cook six dozen light bulbs. In cruel contrast to the interior, Max painted shelves of succulent food on the fridge door, as if by osmosis and the power of positive suggestion pastel apple pies and fluorescent watermelon would magically materialise inside.

There was the occasional meat pie from the Matthew Talbot Hostel for Homeless Men, or a bowl of vegies and rice at the Hare Krishna Temple, although they flavoured their free meal with Religious Fervour. Experts had just deduced that an average serving of dog food contained half the recommended daily allowance of protein and calcium for humans. The carpet in the squat, though overgrazed, had never been vacuumed and was bound to be full of nutritional value. If life ever got really desperate, we could always cut off slices of carpet and boil it up as sauce for our Pal meat chunks.

The rest of our dietary supplement we owed to Marie Antoinette. Pretending to be a representative of the Inner City Runaway Girls Hostel, Mouche persuaded the local cake shop to give us their unsold goods. At five-thirty each day we'd cart off our warm carbohydrate cargo of apple pies, chocolate eclairs, cream puffs, custard whirls, and lamingtons. Pastries for brekky, lunch, and tea were puffing us up and encrusting us in pimples. For a couple of starving waifs we started to look pretty fat and flabby.

Mouche and I ad-libbed life. I basked in her permanent

spotlight. In David Jones, those ecstatic frozen mannequins sent us into spasms of laughter. Everything took on their waxen appearance. The world became a shop window of props in which we romped unheeded.

Over cappuccinos big enough to swim laps in we would draw up our One-Day List. One day I would read all of Shakespeare. Mouche would learn the saxaphone. One day I would write a novel. Mouche, a poem. She would buy a Steinway grand piano. I would buy an Olympic swimming pool. She was going to learn Japanese. I opted for tap-dancing. And we'd become a famous singing duo.

"But not *here*," Mouche insisted fiercely. "Overseas. Australia's so safe. Nothing ever happens here. There's nothing to fight for. No edge." Cappuccino froth formed an albino moustache around her mouth. "Everybody who's *anybody* has pissed off. Barry Humphries, Miles Franklin, Clive James, Christina Stead . . ."

"Peter Allen," I piped up.

"Bruce Beresford, Germaine Greer, Peter Weir . . ."

"Germaine who?"

Mouche reckoned that the only difference between yoghurt and Australia was that yoghurt has its own culture. "Australia's fucked." Office girls glared with disapproval and fascination at Mouche's vinyl mini and leopard skin tights.

"But the reason all the good people piss off must be because all the good people piss off?"

"This country's dead from the eyebrows up. We're intellectual necrophiliacs for bloody well living here."

"We are?" She coloured all my views; my mind was like litmus paper, soaking up her every opinion. "Well, we'd better piss off to London. Earl's Court. It's traditional."

"Na. The Poms are dead too. But from the waist down. They're so squeamish about sex."

"What about New York? In New York," I said, "they have bright-green cocktails and caviar in the Russian Tea Rooms and dog owners have super dooper pooper scoopers and thirty-eight thousand people sleep on the subways at night."

"No shit?" she exclaimed.

And so New York it was.

We called ourselves the Sushi Sisters. Because that's what we sang about. Life in the raw. Uranium, war, rape, unemployment, porno, The Muddle East, President Raygun, Toxic Shock, and Terrorism. This recipe didn't always go down well with the public's mashed-potato-and-peas opinion palate. We leapt out of shopping malls and car parks at unsuspecting pedestrians, assaulting them with song. People either looked down their well-paid, private-secretary noses at us, or laughed and hurled twenty-cent pieces into our hat.

The only pitfall in our schemes was the police. In Sydney, the crime capital of the country, you had to have a licence to sing.

One of life's great mysteries is the way people grow into the opposite of their namesakes. Have you ever met a hopeful Faith? Joys are always suicidal. Charities recycle tea bags. I tell you, if I ever have kids they'll be christened, "Ugly," "Dumb," "Yobbo," or "Brutal, Uncaring Capitalist, Ratbag Carsalesman the Third." Anyway, it turned out that bureaucrats suffer from the same syndrome. To get a busking licence, you have to apply to and audition before a civil servant. He wasn't.

"Your act,"—he scratched at a tomato-sauce splotch which had found permanent sanctuary on his paisley tie— "is unpalatable to the public." He flourished a list of phone complaints his office had received about our risqué repertoire.

"Wanker," Mouche hissed under her breath. He ordered

us not to solicit money on the streets again and threatened that we would be arrested and prosecuted. "Arsehole," Mouche snarled another subtle aside. No, no. We promised. Never again.

While we were enthralling a sandwich-nibbling throng in the Hyde Park sun later the same day, I glimpsed the jack boots and dark glasses approaching.

Why Pritikin diet to look attractive?
Why be fit when you're radioactive?
Unlike the movies, earth has no sequel.
Hey Mr Reagan! We're all cremated equal!

Mid-chorus we flipped onto our B-side repertoire of "Hey nonny no, three gypsies stood, in the wood far lee la nonny no . . ." We were both arrested.

"You're a real arsehole." Mouche dismissed everyone as arseholes. She squirmed out of the policeman's grasp. "Only not as useful." And she kicked him in the shin.

The cop shop he dumped us in was the new one in Surry Hills with soundproof walls and no windows. Mouche demanded to make a call. I slumped in the corridor, steeling myself for prison life—multiple rapes, knife fights, a diet of baked beans and glue sniffing, sharing a cell with a psychopathic insomniac . . . The sergeant who escorted Mouche back came bearing a plate of Iced Vo-Vos. He was coconut-ice-nice and urged us to fill our pockets with biccies before being released.

Back in Oxford Street Mouche sat down on the gutter and doled out our busking money into nineteen silver piles, five coins high, with thirty-two brown cents left over. As I waited for the final count, I cross-examined her about the call. Mouche was like a used tube of toothpaste. Squeeze as hard as you could, you still wouldn't get a drop out of her.

"We're rich," she laughed up at me. Passers-by responded with sideways glances of intrigue at Mouche's technicolour hair. Lately her head had looked like the cover of a heavy-metal record album. She nuked every optic nerve in sight.

"But why didn't they confiscate the money?" We were deep in the heart of Vaseline Valley, so I automatically pressed the walk button with my elbow.

"Oohh . . . watch it," she mocked, "you might get AIDS of the funny bone."

Embarrassed, I tried to turn my akimbo thrust into a nonchalant lean. "What?" I queried casually.

"Let's celebrate!" she exclaimed, jumping up. "Chicko Rolls and two malted milk shakes." She crossed Oxford Street on the DON'T WALK sign and I followed.

And so we passed the rest of the summer. For my sixteenth birthday Mouche shoplifted me a pair of Reeboks, some Ray-Bans, a Bette Midler album, and Edith Piaf's autobiography. The Sushi Sisters developed a cult following and we got a permanent busking spot at Paddington Markets on Saturdays. Our run-ins with policemen made it into the papers. I was rapt to be in the public eye. Well, okay, it was only the gossip column of the *Mirror*—more like the public shut-eye—but Mouche freaked out. Even though I promised not to lose touch with reality, get a dependency on heroin, discover religion, or contract elephantiasis of the ego, she didn't want our names in print.

When the autumn rains came in, our profession washed out. But it wasn't because of the wet that the rot set in. Mouche had warned me about the cockroaches, but not about the two-legged creatures that crawled into our bed.

I stirred from sleep and groped my hand over the sheet. "Mouche?" She seemed suddenly to have gone very mohair.

Mouche's vodka-sodden voice was hot in my earhole. "Sshh, go back to sleep."

The mattress fretted against the sea-grass matting. I

began to get motion sickness. The floorboards were so thin that I felt sure the friction would wear them away at any moment and we'd plummet into Max's room below. The blankets pyramided and fell in time with the thrustings. This had the effect of bellows and sent bursts of freezing air at regular intervals over my goose-pimpled body. Pretending to ignore this two-backed beast, I engaged in a heated argument with my pillow over whether or not we were having a supportive relationship. When the bedding deflated, he staggered to his feet.

"Gotta take a leak." He took aim over the balcony.

"Who the bloody hell's that? I thought you went to the gig with The Mong?"

"I did. But I pissed off to another gig with Sumphead. He's Mong's dealer's sax player from his brother's band. And in the queue for the loo, I met this one."

"Oh, a meaningful, old-fashioned courtship."

"You can bring someone home too if you want to," she offered magnanimously.

Apart from having the sort of face that would launch a thousand buses, this was the eighties. Even if a bloke *was* hot for me, there was no way I would get with him unless he came with a medical. And a reference. "Jesus!" I turned over the pillow he'd been lying on. "You've no idea what he's been up to." I lectured her silhouette in the predawn gloom. "Or more to the point, *what he's been up.*"

"Handle it, *Mum.*" Mouche thought monogamy was something they made dining-room tables out of. "Copulo Ergo Sum," she muttered.

I looked at her blankly. At my school they'd been more interested in the roots than the Latin. "Shit. I just hope you used a condom. Well . . . God . . . At least let me check your blokes out first?"

"How?" she chortled. "You mean, like a mark out of ten?"

"Yeah. On the Richter Rooting Scale."

"Earth-moving?"

"A rooting questionnaire. To complete before copulation. You know, do you sleep in the wet patch? Are you single . . .?"

"Are you an Evolved Male Feminist?" she added.

"And a multiple-choice question. You know, are you a) a sleaze schmucko mushy romantic; b) a psychopathic rapist . . ."

"c) a closet Catholic"

"d) kinky . . ."

"Do you know the Broad's Prayer?"

"What's that?" I interrupted.

"Give us this day our daily head . . ."

Her two-legged leftover returned from the balcony and hovered over the bed. Mouche cuddled against me and screwed up her face in indecision. "One?"

I appraised him in the half-light. "And a half." We laughed and laughed.

And so our pact was made, never to let a penis come between us.

Delusions of Adequacy

Over the autumn months she sampled every sort of man on the menu. It was not a balanced diet. There were the men with ten-decibel snores. The men who wiped their snot on the side of the sheet. (I'd find it enamelled onto the mattress in the morning.) The men with sharp toenails and blunt brains. Some were total grease balls—the Human Chips. Others had their torsos emblazoned with tattoos. Waking first in the morning, I'd read them from nipple to nipple. "Pussy eater" boasted one. "Hate" another. "Consume. Be

Silent. Die," proclaimed a third. Worse than these walking billboards of bad taste were the silent farters. "Orphons" we called them, because they had no pop. They just stripped what little paint there was off the nearest wall.

But most embarrassing was not the act, but the encore. I heard every variation on the lovey dovey, smoochie, goochie, open-wide-here-comes-the-choo-choo-train, little lamb chop . . . pukey pillow talk. "Tell me I'm the only one, babe." And she'd tell them. Mouche's idea of fidelity was only having one man in bed at a time.

Or so I thought.

"Look, couldn't you piss off for a while?" she asked one morning. She'd been realigning her spine in Houdini contortions with some bloke for most of the night. While I was sulking over a cup of tea downstairs, Max swaggered in after an all-night escapade. (He cracked it sometimes, up at the Cross.) I patted the plump belly of the teapot.

"Yeah. Thanks." He pressed the warm cup against his weary eye sockets. "I'm famished. Let's go get some gourmet." We'd often do the rounds of the supermarkets. Demonstration ladies were always asking you to sample little delicacies impaled on toothpicks. You could eat quite well. It's just that it took about forty baby prunes rolled in bacon to make up one decent mouthful.

When we made our bloated return that arvo, I was shocked to find last night's leftover still there. He was sprawled in the lounge room, tattooing a complicated rhythm with forks on the upended fruit boxes we used as furniture. Mouche introduced him as Aussie. He was a drummer with Cockroach Conspiracy. He was also wearing my Eurythmics T-shirt.

"He's wearing my Eurythmics T-shirt!"

"I said he could."

I chucked a hairy eyeball at both of them. "Yeah, well,

don't you *sweat* in it," I sulked. Whenever Mouche went too far she excused her behaviour by reminding you that she was adopted, a state ward, and a Neglected Welfare Minor.

"C'mon Jo, don't be pissed off." She followed me up the stairs and put her arm around me. "How'd you like to be an emotional cripple? I was adopted, don't forget. I'm a Neglected Welfare Minor. I need some love in my life. . . . He's a hot spunk, huh?" I glared over the landing. Aussie was strutting round the lounge room, as territorial as a tomcat. His gelled hair bristled like a toilet brush. I wanted to upend him and do out the dunny bowl. He burped loudly.

"Oops. Must be someone I ate on the way," he smirked.

I looked at Mouche in disbelief. "Oh, he's sensitive underneath," she explained.

"Yeah. About as sensitive as a dog turd."

"He just acts animal 'cause he's *shy.* He told me."

Why is it that everyone reckons they're shy? On every Talk Show on every television station, the Fabulously Famous were revealing before zillions of viewers how basically shy and retiring they *really* are. "Mouche, if he really was shy, he'd be too shy to tell you how shy he really is."

It was when she asked me to help her turn over the sheets that I suspected she may be serious about him. But I knew for sure when she mentioned she may wash them. "I'd be more inclined to boil the whole bedroom," I snapped, doing a Scarlet O'Hara flounce from the room.

For the next three days they stayed in bed. What with no busking and three unfinished songs, we were pretty well broke. He was eating us out of house—what there was of it—and home. And he was always *tapping.* Out of time. Just to endear myself to him, I inquired if he knew what sort of people like to hang out with musicians? I told him, drummers.

"Think it's a snackoid situation," Mouche announced, rummaging in the cupboard and shaking cans up and down near her earhole. None of the cans had labels. In an effort to win a P & O cruise, Max kept peeling them off and sending away thousand-word essays on Golden Circle pineapple, and Heinz tomato sauce. So we ended up with some pretty extraordinary culinary concoctions. One night we found ourselves eating anchovies and steamed pudding.

"No food for you, Mouche." Aussie missed a beat in his drumming solo. "You could lose a bit. Round the thighs." It hadn't stopped him from parting them. "K'niver cuppa?"

"Women carry more body fat than men. It's well known." My hand darted towards the teapot before his, and I drained the brown dregs into my own cup. "All women have those cones of tissue at the tops of their thighs."

"Jeez. It looks like she's wearin' flesh-coloured jodhpurs.' " He lifted his dirty Doc Martin onto the table and began to dig the gunge out from underneath his toenails. It was a regular compost under there. One foot finished, he began excavation work on the other.

"Well, I guess you'll be working all weekend," I hinted darkly.

"*Work?* I'm a victim of the eighties recession," he almost boasted. This guy was a phenomenon. He could talk without moving his brain.

"Oh. You're unemployed." I watched him wipe some of his toe jam on the side of the lounge chair then prod at the meat pie Mouche had placed in front of him.

"I *mean* that I am a technological refugee. A child of the Unlucky Country." He wielded the knife with a pretence of fury. "That's what I mean." I watched him devour his pie. He gave himself a meat facial.

We ate in silence. I saved my olive, marooned in a sea of sauce, till last. Suddenly his fork darted towards me, skewered my olive, and rammed it into his gaping mouth. "What about your band?" I bristled. "Shouldn't you be rehearsing?"

"Bit of a down time for us." He burped and slouched over to the couch with his packet of Drum. "We're not commercial enough. Ahead of our time. Takes a while to get the buzz happening."

What could Mouche possibly see in a creep like this? He even smelt his own farts. No kidding. I watched him. Surreptitiously, he'd lower a finger near his arse, tense, relax, then act as if his nose was itchy.

"Anyone in the dunny?" he said.

"Loo paper doesn't grow on trees you know. We're rationing. Two squares per crap."

"Youse two should sing topless. Then you'd make some moolah. I would. Deadset. If I was a chick." For a hideous moment, I saw our little fried-egg breasts sizzling in the spotlight of some sleaze joint. I looked at him with loathing. Aussie obviously had expertise in one field. High Tack.

"Arms!" I snapped my fingers, gesturing for him to surrender. He reached for the sky halfheartedly. I buried my nose in his pits and sniffed. "You sweated in it!"

Aussie wrenched the T-shirt over his head. "Fuck your T-shirt, you suburban bozo." He drummed angrily on the fruit crates. I glowered at him. He was the complete two-legged Australian male cliché—bronzed, blond, blue-eyed, biceps rippling. Suddenly I saw what she saw in him. That kind of spunkiness doesn't come naturally. He must have been taking handsome lessons. He paused to stub out his cigarette in the debris on his plate.

I examined his hand. "You won't last long you know. Mouche is a sexual kleptomaniac." I grabbed his wrist. "Did you know, you can tell a man's penis size by the length of his index finger?"

He curled his fingers inside his palms. "That's the trouble with you Westie chicks. You're so fuckin' *graceless.*" He leant into my face. "Little earlobes," he snarled dismissively. "Little clit."

It was the beginning of a beautiful friendship.

Mouche emerged from the kitchen to retrieve the plates. Max was hanging off her arm like a human handbag, pleading with her to make popcorn. "It's a palate-fuck," he assured Aussie and me.

"How would you survive without me?" Mouche laughed. Aussie ambushed her en route back to the kitchen. He kissed her. His tongue flickered like a lizard's, up into her nostril. The sight wasn't sensational. It was pornographic, to tell you the truth.

"Fuck the kiddies' popcorn." He looked satanic. Mouche must have spent all night rubbing the 6 off his forehead. "Come on. We're crashing at my place."

From then on, Aussie was the only man on Mouche's menu. And she didn't eat in like she always used to. She ate take-away.

I sat for days in front of the mirror stretching my earlobes, then watching them shrink back into place. The only things I liked about my body were my feet. And even then I preferred them in shoes. What was so radical about celibacy? I had no trouble achieving it. In fact my only erogenous zone was the second shelf of the cupboard where we kept the Mars bars. I stretched out on the mattress and mucked round with a new song for the Sushis.

Why bother with men—they're all married and/
    or gay.
And if they're not, something else is in the way.
He's bound to be celibate, or macrobiotic . . .
Or under hypnotherapy 'cause he's neurotic.

It's the 1980s social disease.
More contagious than dreaded herpes.
Everyone's contracting it.
Right now you could be catching it.
Skepticemia!!

When we got to New York I would eat a mountain of pastrami on rye and get my ears pierced in a place Roxanne went to in the Village, which advertised, "Ears pierced here, with or without pain." This was my plan.

"Have you ever been in love?" Max had come in to borrow some mascara.

"Don't wish *that* on me," he shrieked. "I don't want AIDS."

"Max, you do use condoms, don't you?" I tried not to sound overly earnest.

"I won't get it now. If you don't love them," he elaborated, "you just suck and kiss and stuff. It's when you're in love that you fuck." He grimaced at his denimed reflection in the mirror. "Do these jeans make me look fat? . . ."

"Max, couldn't you . . . don't you like me a little . . . ?"

"Jo, I kick for the other team!"

"But I'm like a boy. Look!" I leapt up next to him at the mirror. "Flat-chested, skinny, and look how hairy my arms are. . . . Couldn't you sort of . . . pretend?"

He wrapped his arm around my shoulder. "She'll be back, mate," he said.

"I make pretty mean popcorn too. Come on. We can survive quite well without her, ya know."

Later that night I heard knocking. No one knocked in the squats. There were no locks. That's how we all got in there in the first place. So I should've guessed who it was.

"G'day, Dad." My dad was wearing his work-allocated steel-tipped boots and best suit. Mum had a newspaper clipping from the *Mirror* in her hand. It was a paragraph on the Sushi Sisters, some crap about "teenage troubadours busking the world's troubles away."

"This is the sort of hovel you'll still be living in when you're an old lady." Mum hadn't shaved her legs. The stubble poked through her beige stockings. "With no one to look after you. . . . Don't you want to save up a little nest egg? Be a *somebody?*"

Personally, I like black sheep. If I were a parent, I'd be able to handle a punked-out poet, or an anarchist graffitist. The last thing I'd want in the family flock is a Pink Batts Insulation salesman or a Commonwealth Bank clerk.

"Are you part of the lunatic fringe?" my father asked me. In an effort to make him more modern, Mum had bought him a gold ingot, and for the first time in forty years he'd taken off his singlet. He'd worn it nestling in his chest hair, up to the Tradies, and immediately got the worst cold of his life. Since then he'd worn the ingot *over* his singlet. I addressed it now.

"No, Dad. Fringe Cabaret."

"Well. Hell's Bells," he said.

We faced each other in squeamish silence on the doorstep. Mum presented me with a packet of new cotton underpants and a bag of oranges, then hooked her cardiganed arm through his. She nudged him. He grunted. She nudged him again, then spoke in his place. "Your father's decided that if you come home you can have your *mattress on the floor!*"

When they'd left I ran all the way up William Street and down to the public toilets in the park opposite the hospital. I didn't know much about Max's night life. I knew he cracked it along the big stone wall of East Sydney Tech, opposite the police station. I also knew that there was some secret carnal code involving red hankies sticking out of right and left pockets. And that Max sometimes put a cool mint up his arse. The same effect as putting one in your mouth, he assured me, "a cool, slow delicious fizz. And no calories!"

"Max?" I hissed. His "office," he'd told me, was in the paraplegic cubicle of the toilets in Green Park. More elbow room. It was dark in there. Feeling like the ghost of Helen Keller, I groped my way along the stucco walls. He was in there all right. Slumped in the corner of the filthy cubicle.

He was manic, squirming and wriggling as I tried to mop the blood off his face. "Sit still."

"I can't. I'm fucking *wired.*"

The sweat was oozing from him. "Are you speeding?"

"Course I fucking am," he snapped uncharacteristically. I felt paralysed. "Has Mouche been getting into it too?"

"Isn't everybody? It's all the rage," he said sarcastically and vomited. "God, I'm fucked."

"Come on." There was blood on his jeans. I took him home. "If only they'd make Mozart illegal. Then you'd be addicted to that."

"I put the snip on my dealer for a loan. I owe him un-tolds."

"Couldn't you have asked him just to give you a good talking to? You can sleep with me." I arranged his ridiculous legs underneath the blankets. "But I don't want you going off the gay and narrow." I fished through his clothing. He could've opened a chemist's shop in each pocket. "Why couldn't you be addicted to something normal. Like a religion. Hare Krishnas . . . ?" He whimpered for Mouche all night. A bad case of the paranoias set in. Max freaked out about people being after him, knowing where he lived, looking in the window. Petrified, I hovered over him, only once or twice forgetting to dodge a projectile chunder. Things had reached an all-time high in lows. It was then I realised we couldn't handle it without Mouche.

* * *

The door focused on me with it Cyclops eye. The electric lid blinked shut. I had tracked her down to the penthouse suite of the Sebel Townhouse, a glam hotel chock-a-block with the Fabulously Famous. Party noises filtered out from behind the closed door. The lifts regurgitated another cluster of multitalented, interstate-type persons. The sort of people who wear sunglasses at night, have sex on vinyl sheets, and boast their individuality while looking identical.

"How do *you* know Elton . . ." oozed a guy with swastikas on his sneakers. "Creatively, or socially?" As they waited for the electronic lid to lift they dropped their own names. I gushed a phony "Hi!" to the guy with the swastikas. Presuming that I was his lover's herbalist's therapist's niece's masseuse he chucked a cheesy. I attached myself to their party and, talking loudly about Elton's claim to have given up bisexuality, slipped inside.

There's less to being elite than meets the eye, let me tell you. The trick is to simultaneously juggle beer, cigarettes, purse, your Human Handbag, and a Lilliputian piece of bread smeared in what looks like dog food, and look, well, *suite*-wise. Elton John appeared briefly, wearing dark glasses. Pointless, really. He's so Fabulously Famous, he'd have to wear a dark bus. While the trendoids grovelled, I surreptitiously slipped plates of cold meat and fruit into my bag. I had never seen so much food. I stuffed myself. I was like a Strasbourg goose. Another mouthful and I wouldn't just have sclerosis of the liver; I would have sclerosis of the whole *body*. I waddled off to find Mouche, lecturing myself that I mustn't under any circumstances tell her I'd been worried sick, or ask where she'd been or why she insisted on hanging around with this Aussie fuckwit.

Mouche was leaning back on a leather lounge, her arms stretched on either side. "I've been worried sick," I said.

"Where've you been? Why do you hang around with this fuckwit?"

Aussie swivelled round to look at me. "Jesus. What is it with you two? You can't even fart without the other one comin' in for the sniff." A man appeared at the door holding a chair above his head. Short and tenacious, he was like a human chihuahua. You know, the type who sinks his fangs into prominent people at cocktail parties, head bobbing up and down at the level of their knees. "Shit! Do you know who that is? Only *the* most powerful man in rock and roll. Elton John's manager. Scottish. Owns fourteen white rollers! Been inside for GBH. Famous for his head butts . . ."

"Does your boyfriend always talk like a Fantail wrapper?" I asked Mouche.

"He's got *ears,* smart arse. He's hot for our band. But like I was telling Mou . . ."

"Mou?" I looked at Mouche, appalled.

"He reckons, to get needle time, we need a chick. Up front."

The Chihuahua was now dangling the chair over the eleventh-storey balcony and ranting about splattering some pedestrians. He hadn't liked the room-service chicken sandwiches. My crap antenna wobbled. This guy was three notches below psychorapist. As he was manhandled off the balcony, Aussie beamed a bionic smile in his direction. "Ah, Sir, ah this is the ah, girl I was tellin' you about . . ." Honestly, it was the sort of smile that would have smiled through Hiroshima. "She's *hot.*" The Chihuahua looked Mouche up and down hungrily. Mouche was wearing white. He probably hoped to sniff and *inhale* her. "Our music's hot, mate! Cookin' with gas! All you gotta do, Mou, is like sing with the, you know, Roaches. . . . Tomorrow fortnight you'll be back in town won'tcha mate? I mean, Sir. Shit, Mou. How many chicks get asked to sing for Elton John's manager, eh?"

"Yeah, but that underarm growth'll have to go." The Chihuahua ran his fingers along Mouche's pale arm. Hearing his voice, I glanced down at the leg of my jeans, expecting him to be there, leg cocked and tail wagging.

"Yeah," chuckled Aussie, "playing hide the pork sword with chicks who don't shave under their armpits is bloody terrible. For an awful minute, you think you've turned freckle-puncher." He flogged the conversation along with a jackhammer laugh. "Hairy chicks. I tell ya! Once a stray pube gets a stranglehold on your vocal chord, you need a bloody vacuum cleaner to remove it!"

I chose that time to tell Mouche about a gig I'd lined up at the Town Hall for *tomorrow fortnight.* A benefit to save the Hump-Backed Tasmanian Tadpoles or something. Aussie looked at me as though I'd pissed on his shoes.

"Fuck benefits." The Chihuahua wrapped his fingers round Mouche's upper arm. His hand was encrusted in diamonds and he wore handmade velvet slippers, his initials embroidered on each pointed toe. "I only believe in one minority group, right? Millionaires."

"Ha, ha millionaires!" Aussie guffawed dutifully. "Yeah, I can *pay* ya Mou." He glowered at me. "That's one up on you."

"One-upping, hmmm. That's a very visual concept," the Chihuahua oozed, running his other hand up Mouche's leg. He was one of those guys who thought he was just irresistible. Success had obviously gone straight to his cock.

"Why don'tcha piss off, ya little Pommy pillow biter," I snapped and pulled his hand off Mouche, who was making kicking-under-the-table faces at me. "I hope your ears turn to arseholes and shit on your shoulders."

Admittedly this was not one of my most subtle and endearing moments. Everyone shut up. The publicity people became absorbed in their ashtrays. Hotel staff were suddenly called away. The Chihuahua picked me up by my shirt and dragged me across the suite saying erudite and witty things like "fuck off cuntface" and hurled me out into the hallway. I would have fought back but I had just decoded GBH. I had a sneaking suspicion it stood for Grevious Bodily Harm.

As soon as the lift doors sucked shut, Mouche laughed and said that she had no idea I had turned into such a Serious Young Insect. I replied that I had no idea she was into Close Encounters of the Grope Kind with Chihuahuas. Mouche explained that pillows *were* on his menu. "Couldn't you smell the mothballs? He's in the closet." That's why she hadn't cared about him touching her. And why the Chihuahua had chucked a mental about being called a poofter.

Aussie had followed us down into the hotel foyer. Leaning up on the sign welcoming Dolly Parton, Annie Lennox, Kenny Rogers, and Lionel Ritchie, we fought over Mouche. I told him he was dumb as an ox and that when he died they'd probably make him into a stock cube. And he called me a suck-back. "Your mother should have sucked you back at birth!"

"Stop squabbling," Mouche pleaded.

Aussie and I glowered at each other. "We're not squabbling. We're in perfect agreement," I said. "We hate each other's guts." Aussie grunted in confirmation.

"I'm not gunna do the benefit *or* the Roach gig," Mouche whined. "I don't want to be famous. Who wants to be known by a bunch of yobbos who don't know you?"

I followed her through the streets of Kings Cross to the cab rank. The Cross was chocker with suburban bozos hanging out for some debauchery. They gawped at the derros and prostitutes and drooled, "Do something *off*. Go on."

"Where'd you get the new clobber?" She was wearing some sort of designer ensemble. Whoever made my clothes was too embarrassed to sign them. I hauled the wheel of cheese from my bag and read the label before offering it over. "Camembert?" I sounded the *t*.

"Camem*bear,*" she automatically corrected me.

"Mouche, why are you hanging with these placenta-heads?"

"Dunno. Get sick of slumming it sometimes I guess. Like to perve on the 'in crowd' now and again."

"In where?" I demanded. "In what? I'm promoting the *'out* crowd.' From now on, it's in to be out, and out to be in, so now that it's out to be in, let's get out of here." Mouche laughed and hailed a taxi. Our trick was always to pick a fat cabbie who couldn't run. Then when we neared home, one of us would cry "Stop! Stop! I'm gunna spew" and we'd bolt as soon as the door was opened.

"Why don't *you* sing with The Cockroaches. I'm not stopping you. Then get Aussie to do your gig."

"Alone? Me? I'd be hopeless without you . . ."

Mouche broke a spoke off my wheel of cheese and sniffed it critically. "Hmm," she adjudicated. "Reminds me of a foreskin I once knew." Laughing long and loud we slid into the seat of the next cab. "Let's go home," she said.

Having Mouche home meant playing host to Aussie and his entourage. The squat overflowed with bad, two-chord New Zealand guitarists, screen printers of political posters, Front Row Forward Feminists, and poets with learner plates who wrote about subtle life-enhancing things such as sperm in the gutter and menstrual blood in the mouth. Artistes Ordinaires.

A few nights after our showdown at the Sebel, Aussie was holding court in the kitchen.

"Chicks, mate . . . have got out of hand." Having eaten everything else, he was now hoeing into the cooking almonds and Ryvitas smeared in margarine. "I mean, take contraception. Mou uses one of them cervical cap, doovi-lackies, right. God!" I waited for him to wedge his cigarette butt in the plate of half-cold baked beans on the counter in front of him. "That cream's so cold. Like dippin' your wick into Dairy Whip. And it's so slippery." He smoked the last life out of it, right down to the filter. "You just get it all coated and whoosh . . . it shoots across the room like a bloody missile. . . ." He squashed the butt into the cold baked beans.

That was when I told him about the new song we were writing, about dud drummers with small dicks who brown-nose Pommy record dealers.

"You know your trouble?" Aussie grabbed my arm and gave me a Chinese burn. "No sense of humour. I'd hate to be the bloke who took you to bed. I bet after a rotten night in the sack, you don't even have the courtesy to pretend." The boys guffawed. I felt myself blush.

"Girls," I stood up straight, "I mean *women,* don't have to gauge their worth anymore through how many you know . . ." Once I knew I was blushing, I blushed more because I was blushing. "*Men* they can score. Not me boy, no way." Once I knew I was blushing because I was blushing, I blushed even more.

"Maybe you're a clit licker," he sniggered. "It's not healthy. The two of youse. In the one bed." He wrung my arm as though it were a dish rag. "She's the A side. Face it. You're the flip side. She'd be better off without you, ya fag hag."

"Let me tell you"—I felt really lonely and sooky and the tears stung in my eyeballs—"if your plane crashed in the jungle, *everyone* would eat you. Even your own mother."

Next night I went to the local dive for deviants. It was downstairs with dags for two bucks. And upstairs with pho-nies, for four. I queued in the cold, waiting for inspection by the doorman. Suburbanites shivered in their Lycra hot pants, Calvin Klein designer socks, sequined caps, and high-heeled jack boots, only to be rejected at the door for being too uninteresting. The dress criterion was charisma. There went my night out.

Most of the people the doorman let in were what we called "Punques"—pseudo or "weekend" punks, who, come Saturday nights, exchanged their St. George Building Society or airline-steward tags for "Victim" or "Misunderstood" badges. Upholstered in vinyl and leather, they also blew their noses a lot to indicate that they had Kings Cross Colds, a snivelling condition contracted by sticking your salary up your nostril in the form of granules of white powder. They considered themselves to be Ultra Now. They were more then than now, if you ask me. As my turn approached, I groomed my aura and tried to ooze mystery and intrigue. He was about to toss me onto the unhip-compost heap, when I was rescued by an exiting trendoid with tailored teeth.

"Hey, aren't you one of the Sushi Sisters? *Are youse chicks on together?"*

I paid my two bucks in twenty-cent pieces and went inside to lurk with the dags in the murky depths of the disco. Pretty soon I was pinioned by a conversational fork prong.

"Let's play carnivals . . ." He groped down my back for a buttock. "Sit on my face, and I'll tell you how much you weigh. . . . How 'bout it babe?"

It was thrills with no frills.

Aussie was down the coast with the Cockies on a pub crawl. Checking that there was only one lump in the bed, I led him in. He fumbled round with my jeans button. "We'll go Dutch, okay?" I whispered, handing him a condom.

My sex life sucked it really did. Well, what did I expect? Hardly any women were transported to the colonies early on. Sheep were the only female companionship for the first

Aussie blokes. That's where they learnt their sexual techniques let me tell you. Many a time I've been tempted to wear my woollens to bed, whack my feet into a pair of gum boots, and lay back and "baaa." I reckon that's the real definition of Australian foreplay—shearing.

It was always all right until I opened my eyes. Then I'd see his chin go all wobbly and his eyes sort of roll upwards and I'd suddenly know that he didn't know who or what was on the end of his penis. You could be a carton of curdled custard, right? I decided this time to keep my eyes jammed tight. That was why I didn't notice what was going on until Mouche started making Academy Award–winning noises.

There are quite a few overrated events in this world. Water beds, weddings, oysters, tattoos, and group gropes. I mean, how can you have a good time when you're desperately jealous that everyone else is having a better time than you? All feelings of mutual sharing and caring evaporate when you find yourself sleeping in the wet patch, then realising that it's not your own.

I tried. Truly I did. First, I stretched over and squeezed odd bits of anatomy. Then I tried to fake satisfaction. I thought a blank stare into space would work quite well. But they were too busy by then defying gravity to even notice me. Next time I was in a group grope, I vowed to take along my novel for the boring bits. Or a crossword. Maybe a nail-manicure set? Feeling like the ham in a most unwholesome sandwich, I fell asleep.

I awoke to find my arm wedged under his hairy torso. I was caught, like a dingo in a trap. He was what was known in Australian Female Folklore as a Dingo Man. The sort of guy who makes you feel you'd rather gnaw your arm off than have to wake him up and talk to him. Not only that, but having rolled towards me in the night, his mouth was now hanging open in my face and he had bottom-of-the-budgie-cage breath. "Pssst . . . Pssst. Help!" Mouche pried me out from under him and we escaped onto the balcony.

"Eight . . . and a half," she volunteered. "Not bad at the old clitoral orgasms."

My orgasms hadn't been clitoral or vaginal. But futile. "I fuck up absolutely everything." I sobbed. "I can't even manage a one-night stand."

"Shit Jo. I didn't know he meant anything to you."

"Get real. He doesn't."

"Well, what's the John Dory?" I shrugged into a T-shirt. "Come on," she persuaded. "Life's too short to be subtle."

"Oh well. Nothing much. My parents hate me. Aussie says I'm a bull dyke. We've got no money. I'm flat-chested with freckles and bow legs. My side of the bed's an erogenous-free zone. I can't even sing. And I'm a total failure. Apart from that, everything's just fantabulous. Tops. Terrific."

"God, you and Aussie are so alike." She dangled her bare legs over the balcony.

"Thanks a mill! You really know how to cheer a girl up."

"You're both famished for fame. Neither of you will be happy till they're selling plastic replicas of your toenail clippings at greasy milkbars up and down the coast. Ugh!"

"Well, you've got no worries about that ever happening. You're not talking to a Has Been. You're talking to a Never Was. I lied to you. I've never even been in a Jacuzzi. Or sniffed glue. Or shoplifted. Or been in love. Truth is, I've never even been to Bali. Or . . ." I blubbered, "up on stage."

"Jo,"—she narrowed her eyes at me suspiciously—"I'm not doing your charity gig."

"Why not?" I sulked. "You owe me one. And you know it."

"That's right, persecute someone who has no parents. . . . I could end up an emotional cripple! Besides . . . we don't have any costumes."

"Shit. Maybe I should just go get a job in a chemist like my mum wants." We shivered in silence for a while. Below us the peak-hour traffic ricocheted up Bourke Street.

"What's his name?"

"I can't remember," I shrugged. "Still, I'm sure it's not the first time *you've* had to greet a man by his pyjama label."

She snorted with suppressed laughter and biffed me good-naturedly. "God, I suppose we could scrounge up some costume ensemble or other . . ."

I snivelled. "Promise?"

Mouche gave me the sleeve of her T-shirt to blow my nose on.

We drooled over the pastels and lace and fluorescent lamé. There was this guy there. His face, up close, was mottled. He looked like a slice of dry, continental sausage that's been hanging in the corner deli for decades. When we told him why we wanted the material scraps, he craned over the measuring counter, ogled us up and down for a few moments, then told us he was a patron of ze artz, and that the shop shut at twelve serty, and zat, if we came back zen, he vould show uz, down below in ze storerooms, ze beautiful zings . . . yes? Mouche and I glanced at each other, our crap antennae vibrating.

Now was the perfect opportunity to show Mouche that I really was as tough as toenails. "Life's too short to be subtle," I said to her brazenly.

And so, at "twelve serty" we returned. The shop door was locked and on a chain. His hand slithered across to unhook the latch and he sidled into the doorway. Sequins winked in the dark. Mouche pointed silently to two coloured silks. He wedged the rolls under his armpit like truncheons. The tape measure uncoiling in his hand, he told Mouche to take off her top. I leapt down from my perch on the THROW OUT, 10 PERCENT OFF, table.

"Go and pick ze materials you like," he ordered me. I could hear the blood pounding through his varicose veins.

"Go on," said Mouche. Reluctantly, I hovered over by the polyesters. I didn't like the look of it. They were standing close enough to brush each other's teeth. Not that he had any. Where his gums should be there was just this vermilion slush. I heard him say something about little poached eggs.

"All ze boyz must keys you like zis . . ." he mumbled into Mouche's indifferent nipple. She must have felt she was being devoured by a beanbag. Mouche baulked at his slobbering progress down her belly. A *sweaty* beanbag. "Just a leetle look." His sausage fingers flicked adroitly under her pants elastic. "An old man can't hurt you." I watched, immobilised by disgust, as he plated her. Honestly, the old bugger stayed down longer than Jacques Cousteau. He didn't come up for air once. Meanwhile, Mouche cleaned the dirt out from under her nails.

I could handle it. I was a Girl of the World. I knew about G-spots and how to pronounce Camembert and which fork to use for the fish, and the difference between Uruguay and Paraguay and the address of a bar in New York where you checked in not just your coat but all your clothes . . . I catapulted across the room and whacked him in the guts. "Perv! Bloody old perv!"

He quickly slid back into his professional manner. "Ze materials." Mouche looked at me with incredulity as we waited. He took us through the tradesmen's entrance. "Vait." He tucked twenty dollars into my hand as we exited out into the wintery city sun.

Mouche eyed me coolly. "You can take the girl out of the brick veneer," she said, "but you can't take the brick veneer out of the girl."

* * *

The redevelopment of our street was under way. One or two National Trust houses would be rescued, but, well, we couldn't pay a ten percent increase in rent. We couldn't pay a 10 percent *decrease.* We couldn't pay, period. We had wallpapered the loo with eviction notices. Some days, as we trudged down the bleak back streets of Woolloomooloo, I'd suddenly feel saturated by the doom and gloom and the grey asphalt. Up until now, my feelings for Mouche had made me sort of resistant to the reality of being unemployed, broke, B.A.-less, and in the shit with my oldies.

Max said not to worry, that we'd all be dead soon anyway. If the diminishing ozone layer or AIDS didn't get us, then President Reagan would. What Max suffered from was Post-Natal Depression—*his own.* He'd always bragged about carking it before he hit twenty. When he turned twenty, he escalated the date of his demise to twenty-five. Max was a kind of dying legend. So, when he did OD none of us was prepared for it.

"Max OD-ed." Mouche's face was drained of all expression. She had been sitting in the dark waiting for me to come home from Paddy's Market. "He's at St. Vinnie's." She slumped into the lounge chair. "Aussie called an ambulance. He went blue."

"My God." The near-to-rotten vegies squelched as they hit the linoleum. "Come on." I stabbed my arms back inside my raincoat sleeves.

"I can't get involved."

"Why not?"

"You wouldn't understand."

We looked at each other. The rain was pelting down. It was one of those flash floods when all of Sydney turns into a large green sponge. I raided Max's dope-emergency fund in the toilet cistern, ran to the nearest red phone, jumped the bedraggled queue. "Welcome to RSL taxis," the electronic voice said. "All lines are busy now . . ." The membrane of the sky had split open. Everything was grey. The Muzak in my ear whined, "Come on everyone get happy."

The next night I rummaged through the chaos of our room and found the parcel of material. Rather than being dazzled by the sensational silks, I winced in disappointment. There was only some boring off-white-cotton. Old fart face had duped us. I cut the cloth clumsily. The zippers bulged with bumps like abscesses. Facings faced out, instead of in. I sewed the hem to the side seam, ending up with a crutch full of armholes.

A few nights later, I allowed Mouche to browse through my blackhead collection. Seated on the floor between her legs, I let her scour my shoulders by torch light.

"About the benefit gig . . ." Her nails dug into my flesh. "It's this Friday, Mouche. Don't forget. We're on at midnight . . . Ouch!" I flinched away from her. "That's a freckle!"

A dollop of tea leaves slipped into Aussie's chipped cup. "Shit," he said. "Don't chez have a strainer?"

"There's enough strain round here already," Mouche's crimson mouth snapped. I slumped into a state of rejection for the rest of the week. Not exactly a brown study. I mean, I still made jokes and stuff. It was more sort of . . . beige.

A week later, with hem sticky-taped and neckline safety-pinned, I waited backstage for Mouche. Love Mum and the Urgent Ring Me's had to go on in our place. Followed by Ms. Cactus and the Pricks.

The organiser was a Front Row Forward Feminist. She clamped my arm in a vicelike grip. "You'll have to do it solo, Dim Sim."

Two caricatured, fishnetted "Sushi Sisters" peered

mockingly out between the big bold legs of the poster's lettering. "It's Sushi," I said. "And I can't!"

"You're advertised. If you don't get out there, I'm gunna rip your arms off, stuff 'em up your arse, kick-start cha and ride ya all the way up George Street." The benefit was for a Women's Support Group. She prodded me out onto the stage. Wobbling on my stilettos—I needed little "L" plates for each heel—I made my way over to the mike. How pointless it had been going to the hairdresser. What I needed was a shop which did Personality Perms and Brain Waves. I looked out into the throbbing slit of darkness. My mouth dried. No kidding. It was like the Simpson Desert in there. My lips turned into Dunlop tyres. Then deflated. I tried to wrap them round the first words of "Panel Van Bop" . . . The first words of ". . . anel . . . an . . . op." I needed new lips. An asphyxiating medley of abuse welled up from the hall. The crowd began the staccato chant for the next band. "Shower . . . Scene . . . From . . . *Psycho* . . . Shower Scene from *Psycho.*" I was, as Max would say, about as useful as an ashtray on a motorbike.

Cockroach Conspiracy's pub gig was at Selinas. Aussie, Moose, Sumphead, and Turbo Tongue were thrashing away at groin level on their guitars. (Headbangers call it having a bad case of Thrash.) I wished they'd just come out about it and design guitars in the shape of penises. "The Cockies' music was aggro and tortured. Early Valium Rock. They moved as if dancing barefoot on bindie-eyes. In the break, Mouche emerged from backstage. The crowd was like a greasy cobweb. By the time I reached the table, Aussie was collecting a fiver from each band member for the Ugly Girl Competition.

"Okay, lob in an hour from now in the lounge. The guy with the ugliest chick wins."

"What if ya don't score?" asked Sumphead. "Any refund?"

"Mate. This is the local RSPCA. This place is full of desperate dogs. Speaking of which . . ." Aussie rolled his eyes at me. "Hey, Jo. Did you know that you're covered in bruises?" He turned to his mates. "From where guys have prodded her with forty-foot poles!!" I looked at him with loathing.

Mouche was licking the lip of a roll-your-own.

"Why do women always give up their friends for some stupid bloke?" I said to her.

She inserted the cigarette in her mouth. "He's my type."

"Oh . . . you mean, he *breathes.*" I flopped into the chair next to her. "Shit Mouche!" She was edgy, drumming a jerky rhythm on the table with her crimson talons. "Couldn't you be more original? It's the total female cliché. The worse he treats you, the more you like him. Pathetic."

"I suppose," she puffed out a cumulus formation, "I have an animal fetish." I looked at her despairingly. Why couldn't she just be into goldfish or guinea pigs like everyone else?

A permed and perfumed cluster of giggling girls wove their way across the dance floor towards the toilets. Arms linked together they appeared like a long, high-heeled caterpillar.

"Shit fellas!" Moose exclaimed. "We've cracked it. A Hens' Night. They'll be hot to trot!" The boys leered after them. Aussie's attitude to sex was so romantic—if it moves and it's warm, then fuck it and count the legs afterwards.

"Trouble with an Ugly Girl Comp . . ." Turbo Tongue drawled, "after a few drinks, they all look good."

Aussie prodded Mouche's thigh. "Booze babe, is a chick's greatest cosmetic." The boys laughed, then lumbered up from the table with Aussie.

Mouche let her technicolor hair flop over her face as she

drained his Foster's. "Why don't you dump him, Mouche? He's a total dag." I strained to see behind her hairy curtain. With bristled tufts and gelled bits, her hair looked like a headache feels.

She shrugged. "He gives me a wide-on," she said.

Checking that the Aussie-Scumbag wasn't watching me, I sneaked into the Ladies' loo. The girls on their Hens' Night were creaming and preening and applying blusher, centre chest, to camouflage undernourished cleavages. I gave them a few survival tips on how to handle the boys and told them about the competition.

By the time I left the toilets, the next band, The Wool-loomooloosers, had taken the stage. They were well into their second song when Sumphead mooched back to the boys' table. "She rejected me!"

"Which one?" asked Aussie. Sumphead crooked a finger in the direction of a plumpish blond girl sipping a Kahlúa and milk. "Bullshit mate! Anyone could get her. God! She's so fat, you'll have to roll her in flour to find her wet spot!!"

"Toxic-shock time," pronounced Turbo Tongue. "Fart!" he called out to her. "Give us a clue."

Aussie waited till she had danced quite close to our table, then swaggered towards her. "Hi babe. Hey, how 'bout a sixty-eighter?"

She raised her eyebrows quizzically, "Pardon?"

"Go down on me," he said suavely, "and I'll owe you one."

She sort of smiled, then turned him into the Living Milk-shake. Looking up from his Kahlúa-saturated clothes, he caught her winking gratefully at me. His face became fever-ish with rage.

"We're going," I told Aussie, taking hold of Mouche's arm. "We don't need you, ferret face." Mouche jerked away from me.

"Oh don't you?" Aussie interjected sarcastically.

The crowd convulsed around us. I tried to haul Mouche to her feet. "Fuck off!" she snapped. In the ensuing tug of war, her bag was hurtled to the carpet, spilling its guts across the floor. There amongst the mess I spotted little plastic jewellery bags chocker with white powder, mysterious miniature Alfoil packages, and a syringe. I recoiled in astonishment. In the music world, barbiturates are easier to get than Big Macs. But for speed, you needed a dealer.

"Where did she get that fit?" Aussie spread open his hands and shrugged. "You're dealing to Max too, aren't you? Yeah well, Mouche doesn't need drugs and she doesn't need you. She hates your guts." I said feebly. Mouche leapt as if she'd been electrocuted and scrambled around on the carpet.

"I show her a good enough time." He raised his voice for the boys' benefit. "If you don't believe me, just chuck her undies against the wall and see if they stick."

The boys guffawed. I hated him. I told him that if ignorance is bliss, then he must be permanently euphoric. I told him that behind every great woman is a man who tried to stop her. I told him he was jealous and that's why he didn't let Mouche do the benefit gig.

"The drugs didn't jump up and bite her in the arm, arsehole!" he hissed at me.

"Don't blame him," Mouche snapped. "I'm ripped to the eyeballs. And my throat's fucked. Couldn't have sung anyway."

"Why are you doing drugs?!" I bleated.

"You're such a fucking squarehead," my best friend informed me. It was true. The only drug I did was the occasional Codral.

"The fuckin' fact is *Mouche* doesn't need *you*. Why don't-cha go back to the land of Hills Hoists and Sara Lee cakes?"

"Mouche?" My whole body felt like your mouth feels at the dentist after a filling.

"You know," Aussie addressed me once more, "you'd make a really good kindergarten teacher."

The one moral code passed on to each generation of Australians since the convict days is never to dob. To die before dobbing.

So many kids were carking it from overdoses that the cops had set up a drug hotline for anonymous dobbers. I went to the red phone. Rang the number. Gave Aussie's name. And the Chippendale address of the Tin Sheds where the band rehearsed. I had one more call to make. Stomach turning, I ran back to the squat, hung my head over the toilet, and talked to God on the big white telephone.

Max was rehabilitating in the lounge room. After the accidental dose was pumped from his stomach, they'd diagnosed a touch of the old heppo and kept him in for a few more weeks. Weird synthesiser music oozed out of his Sony Walkman. Sitting cross-legged, all in black behind dark glasses, he looked like a tubercular bantam. Friends and neighbours queued up on the carpet to pay homage to their punk hero. Personally, I was hard-pressed to think of anything more unglamorous than getting a piece of rubber hosepipe shoved down your cake hole.

Mouche decided we should hold a wake for Max, because he *nearly* did it. We made him a "suicide kit"—a cardboard box containing razors, aspirins, a can of Coke, glue for sniffing, a skimpy piece of rope with a noose on the end, and a box of matches for lighting gas ovens. For slower suicides, we included a university entrance application and an army recruit pamphlet. Hauling the couch out onto the pavement, we waved to the peak-hour traffic and drank toasts of cask wine to people who worked nine to five, parents, married couples, and uni students.

Mouche was nice to me but I could see I was making her irritable. She treated me like a mild case of tinea.

Even though spring had sprung I was depressed. For days. "Smile," Max said. "The world could be worse." I did. And it was. Aussie came to tell us that the cops had arrested Mouche. "Some arsehole dog gave us up to the pigs," he growled. "They raided the Tin Sheds. Mouche crashed there last night. They found a quarter of speed, some fits, some smoko. Took me fuckin' good bong! You know the stainless-steel one? Mouche freaked out to the shithouse. The pigs peaked. Diagnosed her as hysterical. Bunged her into the Psyche clinic. St. Vinnie's. Bastards!"

There aren't many things that beat getting your best friend arrested. One is losing a limb down the food-disposal unit. Another is remembering in the middle of a fuck that you've still got a tampon in. I sat in the hospital waiting-room in a sweat of self-loathing. The Muzak was nauseating. In hell I bet they just play endless renditions of Air Supply and John Denver.

The orderly paused every hour or so to hang up a different sign on the fish tank. NIL BY MOUTH he now exchanged for BED REST. I watched the tropical fish circling each other half-heartedly. Mouche was already a neglected minor. Now she'd be maladjusted as well. The whole episode was bound to give her deep psychological scarring that would surface in years to come. At lunchtime, the orderly parked his pill trolley and rediagnosed the inmates of the aquarium, advocating nurses to "Push liquids." Mouche's future demise was all my fault. Graffiti on Central railway tunnel and lies to a cake shop were just the beginning. Next it would be fraud, arson, terrorism!

Flicking through a copy of *Cleo,* I came across the concluding episode of Roxanne with the hungry thighs. I read on ravenously. . . . But all her dare-devil problems were solved by simply marrying a Prince Credit Card Charming with a blow wave. On the page opposite was a "Are You Plugged into Life?" questionnaire. I wasn't. My score on "How Good a Friend Are You?" was 0–2. Why had I done it? I mean, why manufacture situations that will make you feel guilty? What with the extra hole your spray-can deodorant made in the ozone layer, the vegies and chops you left on your plate despite the starving millions, the time you kissed that man in the dark and didn't tell him about the cold sore . . . a girl feels guilty enough *already,* right?

The next test revealed that I had a low sexual IQ. It was true. Sixteen and a half, and not only hadn't my breasts got their act together yet but I still had blackheads. While Mouche conducted anatomical orienteering courses for alternative erogenous zones (between the toes, interior of nostrils, upper eyelid), I only ever did it in the missionary. Only once had I found myself contorted into a Japanese erotic love position, and then I worried about the chiropractor's bill. It was time to face facts. I had had a complete personality bypass.

Mouche was lying there, all pale against the pillow. "Madeira cake, that's what they fed me on for two days. Madeira cake and Mandrax." There was a chart at the foot of the bed, with a blue Himalayan mountain range pencilled across it.

"I've had a personality bypass," I confessed.

"What's worse,"—she was cold and coming down— "the whole hospital's full of women. Shit. It's like Tampon Towers."

The room was overheated. I was sweating. Now I knew what a chicken must feel like in a microwave. "Mouche, there's something I have to tell you . . ." Mouche was restless, rolling from one side to the other. But before I could confess, the door swung inwards. I was bustled away from the bed. What do you call a group of doctors? A brace? A clutch? A gaggle, judging by the way they grovelled after the man in the suit who was with them. Talk about gravel rash of the knees.

He was an MMM (Middle-aged Married Man) with, no doubt, pinstriped morals to match. I could smell the doses of pool chlorine and see the manicured lawns. The sort of wet conservative who thinks the Western suburbs is just Double Bay—without the view. A Dividend Bludger. His face was vaguely familiar. But we weren't up on current affairs in the squats. Not just because Mouche had banned newspapers. We were a television generation. Without a telly.

He hurled his briefcase so that it thudded into the armchair next to me. "Eveline!" he said. I gasped.

"Dad," she replied. I gasped again.

"When are you going to grow up? Do you realise what this would do to me if it got out in the papers?"

"Dry up, Dad," she said simply.

"What's more, I'm getting sick of rescuing you." Mouche then told her father to get fucked. I froze. "I thought you'd have grown out of this Bohemian stage by now. When are you going to go to university. I could organise any uni, any course in the country. I could buy you a little inner-city terrace. And then you could be a *someone.*" A nurse brought us in some Madeira cake and coffee. Mouche's dad paced the room. He didn't really walk, he sort of cruised, his hands on his belt buckle as though it were the steering wheel of a large P & O ocean liner. He berthed beside me briefly. "You must be Eveline's new friend," he said to me. "You live in that intriguing little squat of hers too, I suppose? Do you see it as a statement against the landlord classes?"

"Um . . ." Bewildered, I glanced at Mouche. "It's a bit of a perk really."

"Eveline's going through her finding-herself stage." He paused in front of the mirror to redrape his hair over his bald patch. "I was young once, you know." I accepted this revelation calmly. "I went high at university," he said reasonably. "Used to really get on my face in fact . . ."

"Off! Off! Dad, it's *off* your face," Mouche screeched from the bed.

"Being antiestablishment and rebellious . . . it's all a part of growing up." He dispensed a few synthetic smiles and handed her a hundred-dollar bill. Then, with his little flotilla of brownnosers all around him, he cruised down the hall, into the lift, and left in his Commonwealth Getaway Car.

I looked at Mouche.

"Shit. Well, I may as *well* be parentless. Don't look at me like that." She grimaced. "Sure! He'd give me anything. But I live on a shoestring. Just like you. Well, don't I?"

I looked at the money he'd left on the steel cabinet. I thought of the new clothes she sometimes arrived home wearing. The mysterious money for mikes, a snare drum for Aussie, taxis, tea out. I thought of how her Australian nasally rasp occasionally lapsed disconcertingly into polished tones. You could positively hear the Brasso. Now it all became clear. The odd crossed *t* and *ing* and *h* were the residue of growing up rich. "You live on a *Gucci* shoestring, *Eveline.*"

"Yeah, well I pissed him off didn't I? He's such a wanker."

"You know what? There's nothing wankier than sitting around calling everybody a wanker." As I ran down the white corridor, the sign on the fish tank read DO NOT DISTURB.

And so I did the most drastic thing I'd ever done. I committed suicide. The first job was making bathplugs in a factory.

It wasn't the noise that killed me, but the Repetition Strain Injury to the brain. The second job was proofreading the telephone book. All those names that sounded like gastric complaints. Next I was hired as a buxom wench in the Argyle Tavern, and fired the same day because I wasn't. Then Max got me a job taking "Fantasy Phone Calls." Being the '80s, business was booming. Long-Distance Sex. You can't dial a disease, right?

"American Express number?" I asked clinically. "Name? Address?" With all the details catalogued, all you had to do was have an asthma attack down an anonymous earhole. "What are you wearing?"

"Oh . . ." squeaked a male voice over the line, "I'm wearing me blue singlet . . . but, but . . ." there was an embarrassed croak, "that's all."

"Well, I'm wearing . . ." I glanced down at my sloppy Joe, grubby shorts, and sockless, battered Reeboks, "leather peek-a-boo bondage gear, fishnets, and stilettos, and" I added, rolling my eyes at Max who, with phone cradled between shoulder and chin, was cutting his toenails, "I feel really horny."

Headquarters was an ordinary-looking terrace in Pyrmont. Plastered around the lounge-room were pictures of groin-thrusting male bodies. "Mood setters," the manager called them. There was a bedroom for long, superdeluxe, superexpensive, or bondage calls. On automatic erotic pilot, the women, mostly housewives and students, could talk dirty while simultaneously polishing their silver, shaving their legs, darning socks, painting nails, ironing, and, for the mums who lived nearby, dicing carrots for the evening minestrone.

"My mouth is now moving down towards your hard cock . . ." I whispered hoarsely, then sprayed out a jet of Fabulon onto the frilled neck of Max's shirt. Max called to me did I want milk in my cuppa? I nodded, stifling a yawn as I reached my asthmatic crescendo. Leaning down into our washing basket, I caught my reflection in the hallway mirror. My dishevelled hair was knotted into a bunch at the back of my neck. My legs hosted three days' worth of stubble and there was an ingrown hair festering at knee level. I was two-tone—albino on the front and scarlet on the back, from where I'd fallen asleep on the beach. The voice on the end of the phone gasped for me to keep going. "Please love . . ." he whined. "What are you doing now?" I suddenly felt sick. A case of Call-Us Interruptus. What was I doing here? Life *wasn't* too short to be subtle. I smoothed my hair out of my face. "I'm doing the ironing," I confessed.

I finally found my illustrious niche in the workplace—Dog's Body. I was a gopher in an advertising agency. These were the Beautiful People. The men were all salon-tanned and the women wore two-inch-long acrylic talons. I spent most of my time wondering how they changed tampons without committing seppuku. The whole office was busy running things past each other, blue-skying ideas and asking one another where they were coming from. (The Eastern suburbs, regrettably.) They had secret meetings to discuss what sort of tissue strength was required to prevent sneeze spray landing on neighbours' ear lobes and the texture people preferred on their arseholes. By brownnosing the nerds who worked in the travel agency next door they got the pick of all the international courier jobs. So, to make it worse, they were always place-dropping.

It was a wonderfully challenging vocation. I made the decaffeinated coffees, shopped for their unsalted peanut butter, whole wheat sandwiches, and dental floss, fed car metres, and collected the courier assignments. I was suffering severe Mouche withdrawal. She had been staying with her father in Canberra. It was during my fourth week with-

out her that Aussie sauntered into the office. Seeing him
again was like stepping onto an old bit of used chewing gum.
He cringed at my supergloss high-tech surroundings.

"How's Mouche?"

"What's it to you?" I tried the verbal equivalent of scraping him off the sole of my shoe.

"You haven't heard from her either, then!" he deduced
triumphantly.

"Your attitude to women is Neanderthal. In fact, if your
attitude had arms they'd be hairy and dragging along on the
ground." I was getting flustered.

"Look, I never said my feminist consciousness was fucking evolved. It's evolve-fucking-*ing!* It's an ongoing thing,
right?"

I filed the latest research dossier which proved conclu-
sively that strength was more important than texture when
selecting toilet tissue. It had cost them eighty-six thousand
dollars to find out that people did not like their fingers
tearing through.

"We need her for the band," he snapped. "Everyone
reckons we're selling out. She'd give us street credibility.
She's just yawned in the face of every talent scout in Sydney. But if you threw a tanty or two she'd do it, I reckon."
He hawked, stretched the phlegm between his tongue and
teeth, then dragged the snot backwards up his throat. I
waited for his Technological-Refugee-Child-of-the-Reces-
sion routine. *"She's* had everything. On a fuckin' platter. *I'm*
a child of the recession. A technological refugee."

"Look . . . I've given up the music world."

"She won't fuckin' well do it without you."

"From now on the only thing I want to tune in is a telly."

"You don't realise the sort of promo flak and stuff we
could put out. . . . Haven't you sussed who her old man is?"

The ad agency subscribed to every Australian newspaper

and magazine publication. Back copies were piled precariously behind us. Aussie scrambled to the top of the *Heralds*, flicked through today's, then yesterday's, wrenched out a page, staggered down, and shoved the paper in my face. Mouche's dad was pictured on the steps of Parliament House proclaiming that he spoke on behalf of the cabinet in declaring his support for the prime minister's view that marijuana should not be legalised.

As I slammed the drawers of the filing cabinet, I told Aussie where I kept him filed—under *D* for deadshit. And cross-referenced under *C* for chauvinistic creep-features.

"Pretty fuckin' weird 'eh, Mouche gettin' picked up by the cops, don't you think?"

"Na . . ." I stammered.

"I mean, nobody knew we were practising at the Tin Sheds. Nobody but us and her . . . and you. Do you know what they do to dobbers . . . inside? Flush their heads down the dunny." He flung his great simian arm around my neck and breathed garlic into my face. "Relax, Jo. The three of us will make a really good pair."

I ran all the way home, like the billyo. The grotty Kings Cross streets smelt like an unmade bed. What I suffered from, but had never diagnosed, was botch-ulism. I botched absolutely everything. My high executive heel (I was on stiletto "P" plates by now) snapped off on the top of the escalator. I was in a hairy situation. If I confessed, Mouche would give me the arse. If I didn't, I'd have to talk her into singing with the Roaches. And then I had no grounds to stop her from seeing Aussie. It got cold. Pausing by the fountain, I absentmindedly investigated a lump in my coat pocket. "Personal," it read, "Courier Documents." I'd forgotten to deliver them to the staff executive. I inserted my finger in the envelope slit and took out the ticket and itinerary. "New York," it read. "One Way."

* * *

"Imagine it!" I gabbled to Max. "L.A., New York. Then maybe on to London, Paris, Rome . . ."

"Great," he said despondently. "Have a Benson and Hedges for me when you get there."

I put my arm around him. We were in the Laundromat, watching our washing go round. "It'll be the first thing I've ever done, you know, off my own bat. Hey! Why don'tcha come over?"

"Sure," he shrugged, banging his hand back and forth below his knee. "I'll never make it anywhere. I'm a reject. Look," he added, "no reflexes. Legally, I'm dead."

"Max, you're wonderful." I kissed his pimply forehead. "You've just got to learn to stop building *down* your hopes about everything."

My toes itched in the showers as I mentally ticked off my list. Passport, yes. Visa, yes. I imagined the tinea tentacles growing up my leg and wished like mad for a pair of thongs. I'd waited till the office was out on their macrobiotic bean-sprout break, rung the travel agency, and, pretending to be a Fabulously Famous Toilet Paper Advertiser, accepted the assignment. Over the last few weeks, I had taken my mother's advice and saved a nice little nest egg. She hadn't said anything against hatching it.

"G'day." I peered through the steam. It was Mouche, standing there starkers. "Got to report to my parole officer," she volunteered. "SSS Day. Shower, shit, and a shave." Each nozzle was in action. She manoeuvred in under my cold jet stream. The bottle of shampoo slid from my hand and spilt its pale blue, antidandruff contents over our feet.

"How are ya?" My stomach was doing calisthenics. "Didja have a good rest?"

"There aren't that many options in the nation's capital." Mouche scooped a little of the blue gunk into her palm and tried to rub it into my scalp. "Living in Canberra is a contradiction in terms." I ducked away from her hand. "My dad has a file on me. I looked in his personal filing cabinet at work one day, under *E*. There I was, sandwiched in between Chernobyl and Financial Summit. All my kindergarten drawings, report cards, psychiatry reports, police record, Girl Guide badges . . . I've missed you. Heaps." She was staring at me. "Jo?"

Honestly, I'm warped. I'm the only person I know who talks behind her own back. Within minutes I was blurting out the whole sordid story. About me dobbing Aussie in and Aussie's ultimatum, and then I ended up saying that she was better off without me.

Mouche lathered up one armpit in silence, retrieved a discarded razor from the garbo, and carved her way through the foam. "I've gone off men." She paused to bang the razor head on the shower floor. "As a genre."

"Bullshit! What are you going to do instead?"

"Dunno."

"Well. There are worse things than celibacy."

"Yeah," she sighed, "like hepatitis and death."

"What about innocent schoolboys?" I suggested.

"Jail bait," she said dismissively. The two women opposite collected their toiletries and left. They'd paid for hot showers. Mouche turned on both abandoned nozzles full bore. As she thawed, she smiled at me. "There's always lesbianism!" The remaining showerers glanced at her suspiciously.

"You can't just *become* lesbian. You make it sound like taking up macramé!"

"Well, it *is* only a slip of the tongue," she said.

Laughing, she started making plans for new songs. A blues number called "Jack the Ripper." A reggae piece on AIDS. A Brunette Spiritual called "Nobody Knows the Stubble I've Seen." I told her then about the courier's job.

She silently lathered up her other pit. "Yeah, well, I've been thinking of pissing off OS for eons. My old man said he'd give me a ticket."

"What about Aussie? You're gunna give him the flick pass?"

"He's a bad egg," she said with feeling.

And so was Mouche, I decided then. Maybe once we were in New York, I could crack her open, sort of separate her personality and just use her rich, golden-yellow bits. . . . "But there'll be other Aussies. I know you. Even a dickhead man is better than *no* man. And *one* man is never quite as fulfilling as *two.*"

"A pact, okay? I promise. And to prove it, I won't see Aussie again."

"Ever?"

She flicked a seaweed strand of hair from my face.

"Ever."

Coiled by giant feather boas of steam, we talked and talked until we'd used up the hot water in all the spare showers. "In New York, they have psychic massage and all-night delis and Woody Allen and . . ."

Mouche had her old man's car outside. It was something sporty with a sun roof. "Wow!" I gushed. "The sort of car in which you can fart with full confidence!" On the way home, Mouche detoured into the Redfern Mall. She pulled up in the HANDICAPPED ONLY parking spot. "You're disabled?" "Period cramp," she winked to me and limped into Coles New World. She returned shortly to present me with a new pair of gym boots, one size too large, some red stockings, a whole packet of Caramello bars, and a cleavage . . . well, a trainer bra that pushed up your tiny pillows of flesh and made them pout over the top of your T-shirt. "Gee," she sighed, "only twenty shoplifting days left till Chrissy."

I began to sing the bars to a song we'd started months

before but abandoned when we'd run out of rhymes. "You're just the buckle on his belt . . ."

"All you ever do is hang around . . ." she chorused as we crossed Cleveland Street. "You're just the buckle on his belt . . ."

"What are you going to do when his pants fall down?" She looked at me and laughed, then slung her arm around my neck. Aussie had nothing over me now, the nerd brain.

That night, to celebrate our reunion, Max, Mouche, and me made gingerbread men, well, not men, but breasts, big rounded rumps, floury penises, and globules of testes. The gas had been disconnected again so the local Italian café, Bill and Toni's, baked them for us in their oven. Max declared that he would get his passport too. "Then when you're Fabulously Famous and own your own nightclub, you can fly me over as your personal cheese-on-toast cooker." While the gingerbread browned, Bill offered us "lemictons" and Tony made "cups of chino."

Beam Me Up Mr. Scottie

I packed essentials only—baritone ukulele, Edith Piaf autobiography, Rhyming Dictionary, Vegemite hamper, and tap-dancing shoes.

It was my seventeenth birthday. Mouche gave me a copy of *New York on $25 a Day*, which was much more than we had budgeted for. And I had a package to collect at the post office. In lieu of a cake, I chomped into the last of the gingerbread testes. They were stale and soggy. I pretended they were Aussie's.

"Cooee . . . Anyone home?" It was Catherine from the parole office. She was nice, voted Labor, and often arrived with breakfast. "Where's Mouche?" she inquired. "I know it's her last appointment, but she's three hours late." I hurtled down the hall. Upstairs, I got out the cornflour packet where Mouche kept her diaphragm. I poked my finger into the cornflour, then poured out the whole packet.

I ran all the way to the Tin Sheds. Students were printing posters promoting the most effective form of personal hygiene and feminine protection—hand grenades. The poet who was addicted to cough medicine was crashed out across a car bonnet. Aussie emerged from the dunnies, a towel knotted round his waist. He saw me and chucked the slimiest ear-to-ear sneer.

"Just came round to ah, um . . . pick up some sheet music . . ."

"I'm not on my Patma," he called out after me.

"You're what?"

"My Pat Malone. Jeezus. I'm not *alone!* She drops round most days. Oh," he smirked, "didn't you know?"

"Bullshit." I pushed past him into the shed. The whole room was a mess of mattresses, mikes, amp boxes. Mouche was lying supine behind the drum kit. She half rose at my approach.

"Now, don't get all shitty . . ."

I faced her, vowing to remain sophisticatedly detached, cool, and cynical. . . . "You wouldn't know shit if you fell in it," I shrieked in a tone usually associated with the castrati.

"Why don'tcha go back to the burbs," Aussie muttered, "where you belong."

"Can't you see . . . ?" I wanted to ask her why she was an emotional bower bird, collecting people that would make her blue. I groped for the words to tell her that Aussie was representative of everything she hated about Australia—apathy, laziness, cynicism, mediocrity. "Did you know that he smells his own farts?" I screamed in frustration. "Didja know that?"

Mouche twisted her dishevelled clothing back into place.

"Don't tell my old man, okay?" The ladders in her fishnets meandered up her thighs. "He'd freak out to the shithouse if he knew I was here."

"Mouche, why do you always have to take the deviant route?"

"More scenic I guess," she shrugged. "Anyway, it's no big deal, Jo." Every word skewered me. "Don't be such a wanker. Besides, there's no way I can ever just dump him, mate." She leant her face close to mine. I waited, breathless, for her heartfelt revelation. *"He knows I pluck my nipples,"* she whispered.

I ran down City Road. Well, I didn't really run, I sort of skied on the dog shit. Mouche was the one who did the Tall, Small, and Medium Poppy scything. Instead of pouring fertiliser on the Sushi Sisters, she wanted to keep us potted, like creative bonsai. At Central railway station everything was bleak and dirty. There seemed to be an inordinate number of derros, down-and-out punks, and three-legged dogs about. Trudging through the tunnel, I told myself that there was a lesson to be learnt from all of this. I just didn't know what the fuck it was. All I knew for sure was that life wasn't fair. It really is depressing to realise that there's only one true democracy in the world. The Brady Bunch.

I collected my package from the post office and studied the scrawl. It was my father's writing. Apart from rationing our phone calls and reusing matches, he had once prevented me from watching a black-and-white movie, *Duck Soup,* on the colour set, 'cause I was using "unnecessary components." I turned the parcel over in my hands and shook it. Mum had only ever received one present from him. He'd rushed home from the supermarket and announced, "Shirl, I've got something for you!" The whole family had assembled, full of excitement, our gold-plated-and-hire-purchased hopes well and truly raised . . . it was a bowel-cancer testing kit. Free. A sample.

I sat in the derros' park in Taylor Square. Knee-deep in drunks and drug addicts, it was called "Fantasy Island" by the cops. Anchoring myself, I opened my birthday package. It was a box of chocolates. Seconds. Slightly damaged. Admittedly half of them had melted, but it was a family-size box. The equivalent, for my dad, of a gift-wrapped Ferrari. There was a note inside. "Come home," it read, "Dad."

Between the tiers of confectionary were some HSC tech enrollment forms. I saw myself for a moment at university, safe, contracepted, with long, conditioned hair and a clear complexion, with a boyfriend as permanent as my hennaed hairstyle. We'd do it in the missionary every night, his sperm routinely commuting to its cosy, ovaried destination. . . . Studying the chart, I selected a coffee toffee. All I had to do was catch the westbound train back home. I bit into the chocolate. It was soft-centred.

The transvestites were queueing up to cash their dole cheques in the Commonwealth Bank opposite. Everything I'd done for the last year had been Mouche's idea. Even my going away. It suddenly struck me that I was going to be just as miserable over there in New York as I was here. Only colder.

Under fluorescent lights in all the grotty rented rooms for miles around, women were checking penis tips for ulcers. Boys were cracking it down along the tech wall. Buying boys was going down in price. The only item in Sydney not affected by inflation. The hustler outside the "Live Girls on Stage" strip club was calling "Gentlemen, gentlemen, point your erection in this direction. Crack a fat or money back." The revolving restaurant on the top of Centrepoint Tower looked like the knob on a push-button toilet. I wanted to push it and watch all of Sydney flush out to sea.

I fingered the plane ticket in my pocket. Two old derros were locked in drunken debate on the park bench next to me. "Give us a fuck, Elsie. Go on. Be a love." Although mouldy Big Macs and sweet-and-sour containers were scattered all over the park, I noticed there was something missing. No cockroaches. This depressed the hell out of me. Trendy Paddington was a quarter of a mile away. The little gourmets had all migrated up the hill. Well, wouldn't you if you had the choice between porridge or pâté? If *they* were up there, what were *we* doing here? Just what I needed. Proof that cockies were a more intelligent life force. So, they *would* inherit the earth, after all. I felt numb. You know. That feeling you feel when you don't? "Just a little fuck, Elsie, eh, for old time's sake?" "Oh, all right then, Eric. But don't you wee in me." I rang the Suicide Hot Line. It was engaged. I looked up at the blue Sydney skies in despair. "Beam me up Mr. Scottie."

"See ya, ya pillow biter." Max and I embraced warmly. I scanned the airport crowd. It was early yet. And Mouche was always late for everything. She had a seven-week menstrual cycle, a seventy-minute egg in the mornings, and had never made it in time to see a support band.

"Do I look too daggy?" Max said nervously, shrugging into his St. Vincent de Paul coat.

"Max, relax. You look great. Just think of all the little vinyls that have given up their lives for that coat. And don't forget. No more building dungeons in the air, okay?" I watched him walk through the departure gate. He turned to wave. "Condoms," I called out after him, heard him laugh, and he was gone, courier documents tucked safely in his swag.

Just as well I wasn't flying OS. I would've had to pay excess luggage on the bags under my eyes. I'd been up all night deciding what to do. Even though this time there was no mother in hot hair rollers pursuing me down the driveway, going to New York was just running away again. Besides, it had hit me about dawn, Australia was *not* the arsehole of the world. Tilt the globe and we were not down and under, but up and over. It was untrendy, but, well, I just wasn't into Australophobia.

I walked through the automatic doors with a catalogue of options in my head. Maybe I'd win the Nobel Prize for my selfless work in the eradication of bad, double-garage band drummers? Maybe I'd drown in one of my own brain waves? I paused to press the walk button with my bare finger. There was one thing I knew for sure. No longer was I going to be wimpy. 'Cause you know what happens when you're Middle-of-the-Road? The Department of Main Roads will come along and paint a great white line right down the middle of you. My post-punk generation had got it wrong. I looked up at the sun straddling the morning sky. I would write to Mouche and tell her. Optimism was not an eye disease.

The Car

"Kerrie, it's your father. I hear you've bought a car?" You stare at the receiver, speechless, like the Lotto winner on the television ad. Your father hasn't spoken to you for five years. Try to remember him. He's the three-piece suit, the nocturnal creature who always vanished in the early morning and only reappeared at night. Habits included putting out the garbage, untangling the pool sweep, and occasionally locking himself in the guinea-pig cage. He was the recipient of all those strange envelopes with cellophane windows. His vocabulary consisted of "No!," "This is my house," and "Who do you think pays the bills around here?"

All through your teens, as you frantically fought for the preservation of whales, women, and wombats, you overlooked one common, or garden, household creature definitely at risk. The father.

You decided at seventeen that with the demise of leather straps and dowries, dads had become redundant. Like tonsils, little toes, and the appendix, disused Dads would gradually mutate and just drop off.

"Yeah, it's going well, Dad," you finally mumble. "Bit of a rust bucket, but it's good."

He rings again a few weeks later. "Why don'tcha bring the car out, Kezza, and I'll give it a bit of a tune-up." Dads of this vintage are emotionally inarticulate. One time, your mum didn't speak to him for a week, served his dinner in silence, and slept on Arctic sheets. Finally, she acquiesced and asked him to kiss and make up. "What are you on about, love?" he queried. He hadn't even noticed. You decode his car conversation. This is your dad's way of saying, "Gidday. I miss you." It hits you then that you love your father. But you don't know what to say.

You visit him on Father's Day. He nods hello, then touches your bumper bar tenderly. He fingers the rust patches and peers beneath your bonnet. "Yeah, top buy. It's in good nick." You chew your nails nervously, waiting for his diagnosis. ". . . Except for the hail damage and the panel beaten back where it most probably had a close encounter with a coal truck." You realise with a shock that you've missed his laconic humour. It's as dry, as he would say, as a Pommy's bath towel. "What this car needs," he concludes, "is some TLC." He adjusts your carburettor.

The next visit, he tightens your fan belt, pumps your tyres, gauges the pressure, changes the oil, puts new contact points in the distributor, checks the level of oil in the differential, changes your spark plugs, and puts pinstripes down the duco. This is the equivalent of a Shakespearean love sonnet.

From then on you talk regularly. Once a week. About radial tyres and rear demisters. About oil and air cleaner filters. About high-tension leads and tighter fan belts. You clock up the wordage. It's a conversational Grand Prix.

It is Christmas when you have the accident. A head-on vocal collision. What runs you off the road are the idle comments about the unemployed not being able to use a knife and fork. And the discourtesy of banning American nuclear ships from the harbour. And then his version of a newspaper story about a feminist who was bashed by police after smashing a window of the South African Embassy in Canberra.

"She was flat-chested," your father declares. He is smeared with cake and clutches a can of KB.

"So?" You detour off your normal discourse. You don't want to go this way. You are like a car in a fog which follows the lights of the car in front over the edge of the bridge.

"I would have clonked her too."

"You mean anyone with small breasts is unfeminine and anyone unfeminine is automatically a lesbian and a lesbian is automatically a criminal? That's idiotic." You both stare, blinded by each other's high-beam headlights.

"You're the idiot, my girl. Living in squalor in the inner city. Sleeping with boys. Don't you think we don't know what goes on. You're the bane of your mother's life. You're no daughter of . . ."

You both sit in remorseful silence. The custard curdles in the 104-degree sun. The grease from your dad's hair has soaked into his purple crepe-paper hat. Herds of Disney deer drawing an armada of sleighs, platoons of caftanned wise men, and squadrons of airborne Santas beam from the mantelpiece behind him. The rellos have departed. The Christmas tree has been stripped of bon-bons, lolly baskets, and baubles. The fridge's white ribs are picked clean. The deserted house looks like a postpicnic chicken carcass. Both of you are sad at the ground you have lost.

"Well," your dad says suddenly. He's hearty now, back on track. His mental Gregory's is open, the streets mapped and marked. "Tell me, Kerrie, how many miles have you been getting to the gallon, love?"

Married Men—
The Kangarucci Cowboy

Kerrie stood in front of the mirror wearing nothing but a paper bag over her head. She looked at herself through two serrated eyeholes. The phone rang.

She acknowledged it with hostility. The look was from a girl to the side of whose head a phone had been permanently attached since primary school. This, she decided, shrugging into her kimono, was how to tell you'd finally *grown up*—when the phone rang and you hoped it was not for you.

"What?" she demanded.

"What?" The voice on the end of the phone echoed Kerrie's, except for its telltale suburban ring of rising inflections. "Sorry . . . I can't hear you. Is that Kerrie? Kezza, is that you. You sound like you've got your head in a paper bag."

"I have."

"What?"

Kerrie unwrapped her ear, shook free her hennaed hair, and elaborated. *"Cleo* said if you put your head in a paper

bag and then look in the mirror, starkers, you can see yourself for the fat, ugly, revolting slob you really are. You
know," Kerrie sat on the arm of the lounge chair and crossed
her waxed legs, ". . . objectively."

"You're not fat. You've got a lovely fig . . ."

"Can it, Debbie."

"I wrap my legs in Gladwrap," Debbie confessed, aban-
doning platitudes, "then go to bed with my electric blanket
on. It sort of sweats the fat off."

"That's disgusting." Kerrie lit a cigarette. She had given
up smoking that morning. "How demoralising. Wait till the
Sisters hear about that one."

"How's Russell? Back from OS? Saw him on teev the
other night and he's looking mega, you know . . . distin-
guished. *Vogue* listed him in their 'Best Dressed Men' section.
He must be unreal to talk to. All those exotic countries he
reports on . . . jeez. Greenland and Chad . . ."

"I used to find him boring," Kerrie nibbled some scarlet
varnish off her thumbnail, "until I stopped listening."

"You're wrapped in him, admit it."

"Russell has one topic of convo. Himself. At least telly
journalism is occasionally an interesting line of work. I
thank God regularly that he's not a plumber. Then I'd be
listening all day to the details of sewerage blocks."

"You haven't forgotten the girls' night out, have you?
Tell Soula."

"Sue's out late-night shopping. Probably gone to Formal
Wear to hire a hymen. Can't get married without a . . ."

"You're so off to her, Kez. She's only having an *affair*.
And it's better than ending up with the latest dag her mum's
lined up. This one's called Petro. He's a big choc, you know,
really woggy . . ."

"I found *Bride Magazine* in her room. She wants to *marry*
that moron Garry!"

"So?" Debbie rushed to camouflage her surprise. "It's about time *you* got serious about someone."

If she hadn't been so depressed, Kerrie would have laughed out loud. There was nothing she wanted more than a monogamous relationship. The irony was that you had to sleep around a lot to find one.

"I don't mean to stickybeak," Debbie stickybeaked, "but ah . . . when's Russell going to . . . leave?"

Kerrie was one of the new breed—brittle, brash. A Best-of-Both-Worlds Feminist, who insisted that the blokes butter their unsexist slices of toast and darn the idealogically sound socks, but also jack up the car in the teeming rain and belt the burglar over the head with the bread board. "Look. We work well together. We go to different parties, cultivate different friends, vote for different parties, fuck different people." Kerrie let her kimono fall open and scrutinised her thighs for cellulite. "In fact we're doing everything to keep our relationship together."

The voice on the end of the phone gave a resigned sigh, then resumed with a tentative vivacity. "Choys. On the twenty-fifth. Seven."

Russell glanced furtively over both shoulders, then darted into the back lane. On these secret assignments he always parked miles away, wore dark glasses (even at night), secured a solid alibi, and never entered by the front door. He felt the keen stab of danger in the pit of his stomach. Russell experienced more terror in the back streets of inner Sydney than he did in war-torn Beirut or Belfast. He stole up to the kitchen window and peered in over the pot plants. A look of bewildered panic passed over his photogenic face.

Startled, Kerrie swung the kimono round her body, one bare, Gladwrapped leg protruding. Russell swaggered through the swinging doors separating the laundry and the kitchen. Known for his R. M. Williams fashions and up front tough talking, newspapers had nicknamed him the Kangarucci Cowboy. "Russell, what are you doing here?" A blush stained Kerrie's face. In fact her whole body had gone vermilion.

"Oh, I can't stay long. No need to go to any . . ." he cast furtive glances at her legs, ". . . trouble." Russell pulled Kerrie to her feet. She struggled to disentangle herself from his pneumatic kiss. Retrieving her mouth, she used it to tell him where to go.

"Don't be like that, pet. Haven't I travelled halfway round the world to see you?"

"They said at work you were attending a television executive dinner tonight." She wrapped herself more securely in the cocoon of her kimono.

"Functions! Dinner engagements! Parties! You don't know what I'd bloody well give to have every evening to myself . . . like you." Kerrie shot him a venomous look then turned away to light another cigarette. "I left early. I had some . . ." he slunk up behind and squeezed her left buttock, "pressing business to attend to." He rotated her towards him and Kerrie nestled into his neck, her anger momentarily muted by a bad case of the hots. "Besides," he crooned, "what would life be without a few risks? Jesus!" He jerked away from her embrace, grasping his neck. "Don't mark me!"

"That's what you came for, isn't it?" Kerrie snapped. "A bit of stomach-to-stomach-resuscitation?"

"Pet, we don't want the press speculating about anonymous love bites now, do we?" Russell's smile suddenly congealed. "Stomach? What's wrong with my stomach?" Panic-stricken, he sucked in air and held in his paunch. "You don't think I'm getting flabby, do you?" Kerrie eyed him up and down as he scrutinised his own reflection in the full-length mirror. With his Gucci belt, leather battle jacket, tinted contacts, and Kangarucci jeans neatly corrugated by Stuart Membery designer underpants, Russell had all the taste money could buy. "At any rate, Kezza, that's not true. You know I'm committed to less gender-orientated relationships. But how can we ignore our naturally strong peno-vaginal-interactional rapport?"

She slammed the palm of her hand against her forehead in despair. It was the late eighties. Romeos didn't romance anymore, they "related." "Oh God, Russell. There is more to . . . to an affair you know than an all-night performance and a well-read penis."

Russell caught another glimpse of her Gladwrapped thighs. "Oh pet, listen. I don't really think I'm up to anything too experimental tonight . . ." Kerrie looked at him quizzically. "Besides," he faked a chuckle, "I think I must have skipped the chapter you're up to. I knew I shouldn't have just looked at the pictures."

"What?" She followed his gaze. "This? Oh." She let the kimono fall open and wrenched off the layers of Gladwrap. "What did you think it was? The Christo School of love-making? I was just wrapping up a few leftovers. Waste not, want not." Kerrie's mouth contracted into a sour grapefruit *moue* as she perched on the farthest end of the couch. "Well, where'd you get the tan?" she asked bitterly. "North Queensland?"

"What tan?" Russell looked at her with wary incomprehension. "Oh, *this* tan . . ."

"You've been back in the country for two weeks and haven't called me."

"It was supposed to be a secret assignment." Lying for Russell had become a reflex. "Anyway . . . Oh look, it was boring and exhausting and I don't want to talk about it."

"Well, you should've taken me too and then it wouldn't

have been so boring." Kerrie flashed an icy smile in Russell's direction. It was a grin that could have come out of an Esky.

"Then it wouldn't have been a secret assignment, babe, now would it? It was all boring business. When we went for a sauna, business. When we sat around the pool, business. When we went boating, business, business, business." He crossed to the fridge and peered inside. "The place was crawling with the polyester brigade. Touristy types, you know?" Russell left the door ajar, leant on it, and focused on Kerrie with the sincere look he usually saved for stories on the starving millions, or a kindergarten kiddie with AIDS. "Is that what you're upset about? My trip to Queensland?" His tan had turned grey in the murky spotlight from the fridge fluorescent. "Or is there some other little thing?"

"Oh no, nothing much at all. You're selfish. You're insensitive. I only see you from midnight to dawn. You talk about exotic women you've had all round the world, straight after we make love." Kerrie launched into a frenzied cleaning up of the lounge room. At the foot of the stairs she gathered precarious piles of magazines, clothing, hair brushes, astringents, facial toners, boots, and books. "There's graffiti in the dunnies at work that says I face-sat my way into television! You confine your affection to times of erection. You have two kids. You don't invite me to enough places, let me meet enough people. You have a wife you don't love, but won't leave." Kerrie shrugged, sweetening her sarcasm with a smirk. "That's all."

Stalling for time, Russell interrogated the contents of the fridge. "The initial stages of a relationship are always a period of adjustment." It was as if he'd inscribed each word in the air.

"Nine months is 'initial stages'?"

Sitting alone in the fridge were two lemons, an open bottle of soda water, some leftover tuna casserole, and an onion wrapped in tinfoil. At least Imogen kept a well-stocked kitchen, he'd say that for her. "I didn't want to rush you. Or interfere with your space, your life-style."

"I don't have a life-style! I have a life! And a boring one at that. You never even take me out to dinner."

"What about that cosy little hideaway we discovered?"

"An obscure steak house back of bloody Bourke, that we can only go to in the dead of night so that no one will recognise you. Great!" Kerrie buried her head in the cushions. It was the unoriginality of the scenario that appalled her. She thought of the hordes of heroines who had draped themselves in their emotional undies over stanza after stanza of classical love poetry. On the passion scale, her little drama was doggerel. Abridged.

Russell let the fridge door suction shut. He read the message underneath the magnetised chocolate biscuit on the freezer compartment. "Women have many faults. Men have only two. Everything they say, and everything they do." He lifted the magnet, letting the message flutter to the rotting seagrass matting. "Angel pie, I understand." He cupped her chin in his manicured hand. "How insensitive of me . . ."

"You do?" she swallowed a sob.

"Yes," he said expansively. "You're premenstrual."

Kerrie groaned and lurched to her feet. "I'm sick of being your 'girl on the side.' "

Russell winced. "What do you want, then?"

Kerrie felt sick. She didn't know. A spasm of alarm gripped her heart. "I want . . ." She hesitated, on the verge of a confused confession, and looked to him for help with the translation. Russell was gazing into the mirror. He held in his stomach, then patted his rib cage appreciatively. Kerrie steeled herself once more and looked away. "To be the girl in the middle. Who was there tonight?"

"Usual television heavies." Russell was only interested

121

in people for what they could do for him. Kerrie had occasionally heard him refer to his friends and immediate family as "contacts." "Bond. Sam Chisholm. Murdoch's man."

"You're kidding?" The names lit up the shabby room. "Why didn't you take me?"

"Pet, it was not a mixed do. It was one of those ocker occasions. It's degrading enough for me to be stuck in the middle of all that insensitivity. It would have insulted you as a feminist. Besides, pet, we do have to keep up appearances."

Kerrie's stomach was churning with tiny unexpected turmoils. "Are you . . . are you ever going to leave her?"

He felt oppressed by the conversation that was about to engulf him. Kerrie, he had always thought, was wise enough not to attempt orienteering in his emotional landscape. "Any decision is subject to reassessment in a different time frame allowing for emotional parameters and unpredictable impactions and . . ."

"So, answer-wise, you'll have to respond to my question with a definite guarded negative." Kerrie had come equipped with map and compass.

"Ah, yes, I ah . . . think so. Imogen is a person in her own right, pet." Russell squirmed. "I would expect you, Kerrie, as a fellow woman, to empathise with that. The three of us have to be above the suburban mentality of possession and jealousy." Kerrie thought momentarily that he had tuned in to some FM community radio station. "In all fairness, my departure must be executed as gently as possible."

"Russell . . ." She fumbled in vain to change his frequency.

"Besides, it's too impractical this fiscal year." Russell spoke every currency of the world fluently. "Is there anything to drink in this house?"

"Cooking sherry. I'm broke. It wouldn't hurt if you brought round the odd wine cask."

Russell flinched. "You know I never drink bulk wine. You earn a good salary. Thanks to me. I can't help it if you're a negative saver."

Kerrie narrowed her eyes at him. "You may have got me that pissy little research job, but I work bloody hard, you Turramurra Turd Brain." She was now convinced that mistresses must have been better off last century. Feminism had created equality all right. Women still got treated like shit, but now they had to pay for it.

Russell swivelled on his cowboy heels to face her. He was torn between anger and an opportunistic appreciation of his delicate timetable. The trouble with women was that you could never just leap straight into the cot. They always needed at least an hour's chat up front, then at least half an hour after the act. Imogen's curfew was one A.M. If he wasn't in the cot with Kerrie by eleven, he usually called it quits. To arrive home this side of midnight would score him some brownie points with the wife. And Kerrie would interpret any platonic gesture as proof of the sincerity of his friendship.

"My God!" He glanced at his Swatch. It was only ten-thirty. "Darling. You're so complex. I can't keep up. One minute I am overwhelmed by the maturity displayed by a girl of your tender twenty-one years. And then the next, I'm reeling from your . . . forthrightness."

Kerrie rolled her eyes at his rehearsed preamble. She had learnt that with television people it was advisable to divide or multiply everything they said by at least one hundred. When Russell described someone in an interview as "fascinating," your translation told you that the person was scarcely tolerable. "The next minute I'm enthralled by your exuberant, nymphlike charm." Now he was combining Gallic hand gestures with his rhetoric. In frustration she hurled herself backwards onto the couch. Russell glimpsed the seaweed clump of dark hair in the crease of Kerrie's thighs. "It's the dichotomies of your personality that make you so . . . fascinating."

"Russell . . ." she flinched away from his fingers, "face it. There's no future for us. You're forty, you know. That's nearly fifty. And fifty is a quarter of Captain Phillip. Your life-span times four is how long Australia's been colonised. Do you realise that?"

That smile Russell donned to accept Logie Awards dissolved on his lips. "No. No, I hadn't realised that. If you find it repugnant that I'm balding, why don't you just say so?" He turned away from her, temporarily eclipsing his face from her view, and checked his Swatch again.

"Huh? Oh, come on. That's got nothing to do with it."

"How would you like to be forty . . . ish, paranoid, in mid-life crisis, unhappily married, the property of the public, and balding. Be patient with me, pet. I came to feminism late. I'm still evolving. When I think back on my attitudes to women. How crass, how callous I was." He slumped into a state of contrite melancholia. "Separatism really would be fair retribution for all my past ill behavior." Russell noted to himself that remorse was not an entirely unpleasant feeling. "I've got a few years left in television and then I'll be nothing but a geriatric joke. A pathetic, prehistoric relic with a hair transplant."

"Oh, come on," Kerrie relented. "It's not that bad." A residue of affection forced a wry smile from her. "Look at it this way. You're not balding, you're just gaining more face."

Russell brightened. "Really?" I'm in, he thought to himself. I'm in like Flynn. "You really see it that way?" He slid his arms around her.

"Yeah. You gain face," she addressed the wall over his shoulder, "while I lose it."

Russell peered into the mirror at his bald patch.

"Frankly, to look at me, would you think I was fortyish?" He was overcome by a burst of tenderness towards himself. "Rasheen, the girl who does my scalp massage, says I have incredibly youthful skin. I'm sorry I didn't call." Russell scanned his mental autocue for emotional pointers. "You know you really are very . . ." he lounged out of his leather jacket, "special."

Kerrie closed her eyes. The summer heat was filled with a sad cicada mantra. The night was stagnant with the vapours of the day—the *Commonsense Cookbook* tuna casserole, the Nair hair remover, the Fabulon fumes, the forgotten vegetables liquidating in the crisper—all mingled now in the evening air, a minestrone of awful odours. She retreated into his familiar embrace.

"You're not wearing perfume are you, pet?" He steered her towards the stairs, torpid and inevitable as a tide. "Your problem is that you're too uptight." Leaning over her body, he set the timer on his Swatch. "Just go with the flow." Kerrie surrendered to her weary lubricity. "Jeez, if I doze off and the bloody thing doesn't go off . . . wake me by eleven-fifty, won't you?"

More Married Men—
The Glory Box

"I only come alive when I'm here with you." Garry yawned and crossed to the phone. He looked like someone who had leapt off a billboard assuring you that Fosters made more of a man of you. His body was the colour of golden syrup, except for a pair of albino buttocks. Soula watched their wiggling retreat.

Anastasoula's mum had freaked out when she'd told her about Garry. "Aussie men only want one thing," she'd wept. "Wham bam, thankyou Mam. And you're lucky if you get the thankyou. . . . They don't know our dances! What will we eat at the wedding? You won't be able to cook for him. No souvlaki, yeeros, dolmades, moussaka. Only McDonald's!" She wanted her only daughter to marry her husband's partner's cousin's son from their old fishing village. Con was mohair and drove a wog chariot. The kids at teachers' college called it a "Marrickville Mercedes"—a red ET Monaro with a sun roof and mag wheels. But the mags were too big for the car. Con secretly smeared the chassis with Vaseline to stop friction.

Garry, blond and blue-eyed, epitomised all the boys who had made Soula's school life a misery. The Skips at school had teased her about being Greek and jibed that she'd never get an Aussie boyfriend 'cause she only had one eyebrow. "It's like a skid mark! Vroom!" they used to say. "Right across your forehead."

"Me," Garry announced into the phone. "Just going to sink a coupla coldies with the boys." Soula sat with her thin knees folded up against her bare chest. "Rain?" He covered the mouthpiece before rolling his eyes, as though this look of frustration would otherwise have been audible to his wife. "Bloody oath," he said into the receiver. "It was like a bloody chocolate cake mix out there on that field. I'm covered in mud and shit from head to . . ." Soula stared across the carpet at the smooth, clean contours of Garry's body. "Okay darl . . ." Glancing self-consciously at Soula, he cut short his endearment and replaced the receiver in its cradle. "She's okay," he said by way of apology. "In her own way." He looked at her expectantly, but Soula had wriggled her big toe under the tear in the armchair and was concentrating on snapping threads with her toe. Garry flicked the television remote control and sprawled back along the couch as the set hissed into life. His gastric juices gurgled and he slapped his muscly midriff with the affection usually reserved for a favourite pet. "Jeez I'm hungry, Sue. Anything to eat babe?"

Without thinking, she crossed to the kitchen and gazed into the fridge. Soula had read an article in *Cosmopolitan* claiming that you could analyse someone's personality by the contents of their fridge. A couple of shrivelled lemons and a carton of congealed custard was all. She made a mental note that once Garry moved in, she would call DJ's Food Hall and get them to deliver her a whole new personality.

"Gail doesn't cook," Garry whinged. "She burns." Soula

chipped her way through the freezer to excavate a packet of fish fingers from the ice pack. "And what she doesn't burn, she thaws." He raised one buttock to launch a loud fart. "Jeez! That packet shit my wife feeds me . . . drop one fart and you're hungry again." Soula abandoned her rescue mission and buried the packet deep within the Arctic wastelands of her freezer.

Garry was positioning a bucket of water between his legs. Fishing underneath the couch, he retrieved the top half of a plastic Orchy orange-juice container. He placed it over the bucket, lit the small tinfoil cone containing the dope, placed his mouth over the neck of the bottle and inhaled.

"Gaz . . ." Soula was constructing pagodas of cheese, tomato, and capsicum. "What do you want? To be buried or cremated?"

He exhaled long and hard. "Cremated. Who wants to be put to bed with a shovel? Besides, I've been buried up to my ears in shit most of my life. Repayments, mortgages . . ." He suspended his head once more over the bucket and performed a Hoovermatic inhalation.

"I wonder if there is an afterlife . . ." Gingerly she lifted her towering culinary creations onto the griller, where all three sandwiches slowly capsized.

"Na. Load of bullshit." He laced his fingers behind his head and stretched back on the couch as if he were sunbathing beneath the overhead fluorescent. "Mind you, I may pack a couple of tinnies and a cut lunch. Just in case."

"Are you frightened?" She salvaged some shreds of lettuce. "You know, of dying and that?"

"Na." Garry flicked off the ring pull of his beer can and frisbeed it in the vague direction of the overflowing ashtray. "I've thought it all through. Reincarnation and death and that. And it doesn't really matter. 'Cause, no matter where you go . . ." he leant up on one elbow to deliver his insight

129

into the mysteries of the universe, "there you are!" Then he immersed himself in a rerun of Dallas.

"But like, if there *is* some sort of God bloke," Soula insisted, leaning on the armrest opposite him, "why doesn't he give me some kind of a . . . sign?"

"Yeah," Garry agreed. Thinking she was finally about to elicit from him some kind of romantic commitment, Soula looked at her lover with longing. "Like stopping Clubbies from dropping in on me and dingin' me board," he concluded. "Arseholes!"

Soula rescued the scorching toast. The cheese had puffed into brown pillows. "But the world is so weird." She pierced the bloated bits with a fork and camouflaged the damage beneath a layer of anaemic lettuce. "Take us for example. Like, all the other teachers at school reckon we're just mates. Nobody suspects that we're sort of, like passionately in love an' that!"

"Yeah, yeah," he grunted, "I was thinking about all that stuff out on me board today."

Soula looked up expectantly. "What stuff?"

"As I got chundered in a six-foot swell, I thought how weird it is to call the Pacific Ocean the Pacific. It never is. Peaceful, you know? I mean, and Greenland. It's not green, it's all iced up. And flying fish don't fly. They just sort of water-ski on their fins. Fascinating, huh?" Garry wrapped himself around his toasted sandwich. "What about you? Haventchagottamuncheeez?"

"Pardon?"

He swallowed. "Haven't you got the munchies?" Looking at her protruding hip bones and concave stomach, he noticed for the first time that his lover had turned into a human dipstick.

"Knowing my luck, I'll be reincarnated as a . . ." She folded herself into a different shape at his feet. "Nun."

He stretched his legs nonchalantly across her lap. "What are we yacking about this morbid shit for, huh? As long as next time round we're reincarnated together." Poised to kiss her, he lowered the sandwich. But the melted cheese stretched like bubble gum from his mouth. "Shit." He dissected the sandwich, *"Who* is it?" and peered inside. "Where are the others tonight anyways?"

"Julia's at her Prisoners Action Group thingo, and Kerrie's out with that sleaze-schmucko she hangs round with. He'll never get divorced and marry her. She'll miss the boat. She'll be an old boiler. You get past being marriage material. I mean," Soula's voice lowered to a revelatory hush, "she is twenty-two you know! Don't you reckon," she said tentatively, "it's off for a guy to string a girl along like that . . . ? You know, exploitative?"

He flicked a copy of *Cleo* off the end of the couch with his foot. "I reckon the only thing that's off is all the bulldyke literature they force-feed you."

He sounded like her mother. "Going to teachers' college will stuff up your brain. You should have met a nice boy at the Greek Club and settled down by now. Men can tell if you're not a virgin. You've only got one bag. If that bag gets filled, I'll scratch your eyes out! *Tha vgalo ta matia sou!"*

"And I reckon it's off that the only reading *you* do is the back of the Corn Flakes pack! You're a Corn Flakes Conversationalist. Did you know that? Like it gets really sort of dull talking about riboflavin and niacin all the t . . ." For the first time in front of him, she burst into tears.

Alarmed, Garry leant down and stroked her upper arm. "It's not that bad," he comforted. "You can learn a lot from the back of the pack. Did you know," he recited, in an effort to cheer her up, "that swans mate with the same partner forever?"

Soula dumped his legs off her lap and manoeuvred a

cushion into the fig-leaf location. "How *is* Gail?"

"Oh!" He slammed the flat of his hand into his forehead. "She reversed into the letterbox the other day. In the god-damned Laser." With surgical precision he picked apart the melted contents of his sandwich. "Loves to look in any mirror, except the rear vision." He glanced up from his dis-section. "Hey, don't forget your bloody car reggo, Susie. It's due about . . . You know the Esso garage near school? They'll look after you. Just mention my name. . . . She's got so slobby round the house too. Shit! What are you trying to do?" With forefinger and thumb, he extracted a piece of melted plastic cheese wrapper and flicked it onto the carpet. "Get my water cut off? . . . Drops her underchunders and clothes all over the friggin' floor too."

Soula groped under the record player for the T-shirt she had discarded earlier in the evening, then scanned the lounge room for her underpants. They were lying scrunched up at the foot of the stairs where she'd stepped out of them. Her mum had refused to show Soula's messy bedroom to the mothers of prospective husbands. "How can you expect someone to marry you if your bedroom's *ano kato* . . . how do you say . . . pigsty?" When visitors came, you scored bridal points for tidiness, serving the Greek coffee and cake and sitting with your legs together.

"She's just let herself go," Garry added through another mouthful of sandwich. With an air of contrived casualness, Soula started to tidy up the room, pausing briefly by the mirror to pat her hair and remove the skid marks of mascara beneath her eyes. "Goes out looking like a dog. Any day now, she's gunna start sticking her head out of the car window." Soula fingered her fresh crop of underarm stub-ble and wished she'd shaved before his arrival. "I came *that* close . . ." he separated the thumb and forefinger of his other hand by a millimetre and squinted as if threading a needle, "to bloody well leaving the other day."

"Why didn't you?" Soula queried airily, as though she were vaguely curious about the number of miles he was getting to the gallon these days. "Did you talk to her about it? You promised."

He cleared his throat. "Yeah."

Soula looked into his eyes for the first time that night. "Have you?" she interrogated.

"Well . . . I forget." Feeling suddenly exposed, he fumbled for his football shorts and wriggled into them. "It's probably better if I let her, you know, bring it up. She had a bad Easter. The Jindabyne excursion. The whole time we were away the kids were monsters. Ben threw his new dental plate down the food-disposal unit. And . . . I mean, face facts, Sue. I'm to blame too." Soula milked the teat of the wine cask into her glass, downed it in one gulp, then refilled it. "She's not independent like you." Soula let out a burst of loud, unnerving laughter. "If I left, there's no telling what she might do." He offered her his homemade bong. "Pull a cone," he said magnanimously. "Calm down."

"But do you like her?"

Garry shrugged. He rubbed his sweaty palms up and down his footy socks. "I'm used to her. And in her own way, she's devoted."

"But *we* love each other."

"It'll get easier when the kids are older. . . ." His striped shins were now quite damp.

"I *love* you."

"What's a year or two when we have a whole lifetime together ahead of us. And . . ." Garry focused Soula with his blue and bloodshot eyes, "maybe," he said enigmatically, *"beyond that . . ."* The lounge-room window mirrored his handsome reflection. He tousled his hair and rumpled his jersey into the "I've-just-slogged-it-out-on-the-footy-field" look.

"Do you love me?"

Deciding to tackle the situation head on, he lunged across the couch and took her by the shoulders. "I want to be with you always. I mean, I really can talk to you. I knew when I first met you in the bloody staff room and you were wearing those shoes with the, you know, musical notes on them . . . that you were, well, different to other women. I've got it off with a lot of chicks spunkier than you, and it sucked. They want to take me over." He tapped his temple dramatically. "You know, owner-occupy. But when I'm with you . . ." he struggled, "I feel as though I'm with an old mate. You're ace, Sue. You're a good sport. I feel as if we're equals. That's it! We're equal. Basically, you're just like a guy!" He looked elated, as though he had just scored a try.

Anastasoula thought about the trunk underneath her bed. Her glory box was big enough to open as a department store. Seventy-five tea towels. Dozens of hand-crocheted doilies. Eighteen vegetable peelers. Quilted bedspreads. Two sets of crockery. Sterling-silver cutlery in large velvet boxes. Coloured Tupperware contraptions for straining, sealing, shredding. For the last two hours she had also been thinking about swallowing a bottle of Seconal, lying down in the box, and closing the lid.

Garry emptied the bucket into the withering pot plant, delved into the mud, mixing it into the desired chocolate cake consistency, then smeared his limbs. "Hate to eat and run, but better make tracks. Gail's getting a bit sus of footy training five times a week for an amateur club." He flashed a conspiratorial smile in her direction. "I can pop in for . . . 'coffee,'—he slid open the side alley window—"Wednesday." His buttocks balanced on the sill, he continued, "Around midnight." With a one-finger salute, he hurtled onto the nasturtiums in the garden below.

Soula stood gazing after him. Postmatch depression set in. She was the losing team, vanquished, left knee-deep in chip and pie wrappers. It was against Greek Orthodox religion to commit suicide. They wouldn't bury you. It was almost as bad as being an old maid. And what would her relatives say? Aunty Toula, Aunty Voula, Aunty Koula, Aunty Roula? *Christémou!* As if she weren't in enough shit with her mother already.

"Susie!" Garry's head catapulted back through the window to deliver a passionate postscript.

"Yes!" Her heart leapt. Soula had not yet caught up with the eighties fashions. If you wear your heart on your sleeve, wear a cardie.

"Why don't you watch *Alf* tomorrow night? Then I can think of you while I'm watching it with the kids. *Ciao!*"

More or Less Married Men—Girls' Talk

The Darlinghurst terrace was filled with the paraphernalia of three single girls. Ailing pot plants, posters, piles of magazines, were crammed amongst Kerrie's collection of Aussie kitsch—they poured their tea from a china kangaroo, ate their eggs from Ayres Rock egg cups, and rested their drinks on kangaroo-fur coasters. The permanently erected ironing board, rusted into a state of rigor mortis, doubled as a coffee table. Washing withered on a makeshift line in the bathroom. Above the kitchen sink hung a map of Australia from which Queensland had been cut off and set adrift towards the flaking ceiling. The fridge door was smothered with appetite-deterring photos of magazine models with mocking smiles.

A spunk chart with piccies of favourite men was pinned up behind the bathroom door. In random order were Sam Neill, Sean Penn, Spike Milligan, The Mean Machine, Michael Hutchence, Garibaldi, Lord Byron, Bill Murray, and Bette Midler (the only woman, all three agreed, who could make them turn).

By the stove was the Knee-Capping Top Ten—various fascists and landlords, but most of them were married men.

"I gather neither of you is doing any animal husbandry tonight? I haven't sat on Arctic porcelain all afternoon." Julia was fastidiously clipping her toenails. "That's the only way I ever know if either of your revolting blokes is in the house—if the toilet seat's up."

Kerrie, bottle blond and just back from a day's baking on the nudist beach, rolled her eyes and turned to Soula in a tone of forced airiness, "How *is* Garry?"

"Oh fantastic! Tops . . . But now Mum and Dad are trying to pair me off with Costa. He's a total soccer-head. . . . How's Russell?" Soula reciprocated.

"Oh excellent. As romantic as ever!" Kerrie said, nodding.

They both stared dismally at the nail clippings Julia was collecting on the TV guide. It was Saturday night.

"Celery?" Kerrie said abruptly, thrusting a plate of wilting greens towards Julia.

"Dunno why you both bother with men." Julia, who had begun the afternoon at a drunken book launch for anarchist poets, topped up her friends' glasses. "It'd be much easier just to masturbate."

"Is *that* what you do? Of course." Kerrie's face, caked in an organic avocado face mask, had a gangrenous pallor. "That's what you believe in, isn't it? Sex with someone 'idealogically sound.' "

"Lay off, Kerrie. You're embarrassing." Soula was rubbing a Silkymit over her legs. "You don't, do you, Jules?" she said, disappearing in a cloud of white powder.

"Wanking does have its good points, Sue," Kerrie said through a mouthful of vegetable matter. "You don't have to shave your legs or depube first." Kerrie revelled in being scandalous. She didn't just lampoon sacred cows, she milked them dry, then barbecued them.

Soula held both legs out in front of her to check she hadn't whittled one leg thinner than the other. "Anyway, I reckon men don't respect a woman who's too shop-soiled," she said as if possessed of some secret inner knowledge. Kerrie and Julia stared at her in stupefaction. Along with the girl-eating roaches and rising damp, Soula had been inherited when they moved into the house.

"Good, Sue," Kerrie pronounced, munching a carrot. "Look, why don't you go squeeze a blackhead or something."

"You've desensitised yourself, Kerrie, did you know that?" Julia spoke slowly and emphatically, in time with her clipping. A bit of toenail shrapnel ricocheted across the room. "You've become just like men." Soula turned on the television.

"Me! I'm not like men. You are. Leaning up against the bar with your Front-Row-Forward-Feminist Mates." Soula pressed her hands over her ears. "All with cropped hair and boiler suits, swearing and beer swilling and backslapping and calling each other 'mate.' Kerrie's facial exertions cracked the green contours of her mask.

"Well," Julia retorted, *'you're* no better than Tracey— servicing the whole bloody football team. *You* think promiscuity is feminism. Only the men are laughing all the way to the sperm bank!"

Soula let out a desolate sob. Kerrie and Julia swapped exasperated grimaces.

"Come on," Kerrie relented. "It's not all that bad. You might be a wimp, but at least you're not ugly and fat. Look at *that.*" She lifted the limp elastic of her Speedos and pinched a roll of thigh between finger and thumb.

"It's called skin," Julia admonished. "You need it to bend and sit with."

"I can do better than that." Soula snivelled, dropped her floral shorts, and struck a similar pose. "Look at that!"

"But yours doesn't go all wrinkly and squelchy when you squeeze it," Kerrie said triumphantly. "Look!"

"At least," proclaimed Soula, gulping her glass of wine, "neither of you is ugly and hairy and have to worry about VHL."

"You think *you're* ugly . . ." Kerrie began, then paused perplexed. "VHL?"

Soula ran a finger along the lacy edge of her bikini pants. "Visible Hair Line," she whimpered.

Kerrie inspected the groin of her inebriated girlfriend. "Wow! Neck-to-knee pubes. You know how scientists reckon there's a missing link between the primates and modern man?" she joked. "Well, it's you!" Soula's face fell. "Come on," Kerrie comforted. "You're Greek, for God's sake!"

"At least you don't have big tits," Julia said brightly. "You can pass the pencil test."

"The what?" Kerrie watched as Julia unhooked her bra, threaded her arms through the straps, and flung the bra on the floor. Lifting up her T-shirt, she placed a pencil in the cleft beneath her bosoms. It sat there, clenched in the crevice.

" 'The Dreaded Droop,' " she sighed, her self-righteousness diluted by the camaraderie and the wine cask.

"Gimme." Kerrie tried it. The pencil slid to the carpet. Julia shot her friend a look of mock disgust.

"At least you've got tits. Look." Soula hitched up her T-shirt. "Mozzie bites."

"More than a mouthful," Kerrie declared, "is a waste."

All three collapsed in front of MTV, where a groin-thrusting group was shrieking about carnal ecstasy.

"Who needs men anyway?" Julia proclaimed. "What with AIDS, more and more people are turning to abstinence."

"Yeah, well I'm allergic to all diets," Kerrie muttered. "I

betcha scientists discover one day that celery was fattening all along."

"Don't worry," Soula said rapturously as she crossed to the kitchen. "I read this article in *Cleo* and apparently you can sort of translate emotional reactions like aggro, nervous breakdowns, and tanties and stuff into calories burned." She shovelled a slab of Sara Lee into her mouth. "The more like miserable we get the more calories we're losing!"

"I should be anorexic, then," Kerrie said, stacking a tray with pecan pie, lamingtons, a carton of ice cream, three spoons, and a packet of Tim Tams.

"It's disgraceful that we worry about such superficialities." Julia deposited her toenail clippings in the kitchen tidy. "Not being 'beautiful' has forced us to develop other assets—brains, personality, charm . . ."

"Modesty," Kerrie added through a mouthful of carbohydrates.

"Yeah," Soula said with animation, "Garry reckons that beauty shines from within. That your, you know, inner aura, like seeps through?"

Kerrie and Julia nodded encouragingly while rolling their eyes at each other.

"Anyway," mumbled Kerrie, licking the chocolate layer from a Tim Tam. "None of us is overweight. We're just . . ." she shrugged, *"under* height."

"Besides, being fat, hairy, and ugly are great qualifiers. I mean," Julia slurred, "who'd be interested in a man if he wouldn't be interested if you were fat, hairy, or ugly?"

"Yeah. I don't know why we let ourselves get so fussed about men." Kerrie had begun to pluck her eyebrows, her speech interrupted by the occasional volley of sneezes. "All they ever do is burp and fart."

"It's Mexican that sets Gaz off," Soula giggled. "And he always drops them in the car!"

The three friends snorted.

"And you know what else? He makes me, like, lie down in the backseat in case anyone from school sees us."

"You think that's bad. D'ya know what Russell said to me the other night? 'Do you mind not coming when I'm coming? I find it distracting . . . I'll tell you when I'm about to come and you just hold really still.' "

"You're joking!" Julia and Soula exclaimed.

"Na. Deadset . . . So there I was, clinging to the sheet, straining for the cue, when suddenly it hit me that, shit, if my presence was distracting, then who did he think was on the end of his dick. . . . Or worse, *what?* I could've been a dead shark! Russell sucks." Kerrie ground the words out as she texta-ed his name onto the Knee-Capping Top Ten. "I'm sick of being treated like shit. I'm going to piss him off and let something tall, dark, and handsome happen to me. And *I'll* be calling the shots. You bet! Things *have* changed. We won't be done over like our poor old mums. We don't have to lie back and think of England!" Kerrie was now parading round the room.

"Exactly," Julia said approvingly. "It's better to have loved and lost . . . than to spend your Saturday nights pining for a married man."

"Yeah. I'm going to like lay it on the line with that sleaze schmucko Garry. He either leaves home and marries me, or I'll dump him."

"We'll have their balls for breakfast!" Julia enthused.

"We'll trample on the piss ants!" Kerrie stamped her foot.

"Men. Who needs 'em!" Soula cheered.

A knock echoed down the hallway. The three women froze. Kerrie and Soula leapt to their feet as if stung. Kerrie chipped at her face mask. Soula dusted off her legs. Kerrie buried the biscuits behind a pillow on the lounge. Soula flicked the elastic out of her hair and ruffled it into a nonchalant I-don't-care-about-my-hair look. Kerrie smeared Russell's still-wet name off the Knee-Capping Top Ten. Soula groped, terror-stricken, beneath her armpits.

Julia surveyed the bedlam, dumbfounded.

"Shit!" the two girls chorused. "Stall him, Jules! Stall him!"

Kerrie bolted towards the bathroom, bowling Soula out of the way. "Where's my diaphragm?"

"Shit," Soula shrieked, "I have to shave my pits!" She sprinted down the hallway after Kerrie.

Julia looked at the deflated wine cask. "Yeah," she muttered. *"Sure,* things have changed! Now we just lie back and think of Canberra . . ."

The Ned Kelly Complex

I suppose my cause has always been causes. My friends have survived my fads. They've had dinner with the UNESCO expert on world famine who ate all the after-dinner mints. They invited the vegetarian activist on our Bondi Beach barbie and didn't flinch when the all-girl Melbourne rock band, the Black and White Menstruals, moved in for two days and stayed two months.

But Billy was different; I was convinced that he was more than a hobby.

I met him on a journalistic assignment: maximum-security jails for men. My tape recorder set the metal detector wailing. The contents of my bag were searched: novel, antinuclear pamphlets, uncashed cheques, lollies covered in fluff, condoms, emergency Meds, bus tickets, invitations to book launches and the suburban weddings of school friends, unpaid parking fines . . . nothing you'd ever see in the ads for Glomesh handbags. I was told to wait with the other visitors.

The women looked vaguely familiar. In their early to

mid-twenties, they wore bright designer jumpers, big earrings, leather skirts, overalls, and T-shirts emblazoned with
slogans. One well-endowed chest read THE JAILS ARE THE
CRIME. Another promised TODAY'S PIGS would be TOMORROW'S
BACON. I realised with a start that they looked a lot like me.
The auditorium was wall-to-wall men. The Beast, Mag-
pie, Bruce the Tooth. There was a subdued violence about
their cracking of knuckles, thumb-twiddling, and knees that
jiggled up and down like teabags. Beneath the cheap prison-
issue soap and aftershave, there was also a certain smell
about them. A hungry smell. Five or six of them swarmed,
piranhalike ready to ravage each female.

The topic for today's debate was "Conjugal Rights for
Long-term Prisoners." The murmurous crowd used the discussion as camouflage for kissing and the smuggling of contraband. But the final speaker caught their attention. The
whole auditorium reeled from the whiplash of his voice. He
was passionate, angry, articulate. His speech swung from
breathtaking bravado to a luminous gravity. Though pep-
pered with words like *oleaginous* and *persiflage,* his sentences
were chock-a-block with *I seen* instead of *saw, brought* for
bought and an abundance of *brungs.* As he spoke, he slowly
centred his gaze on me.

"This is Billy. Billy Bridges. Better known as 'The
Mouth,'" Bruce the Tooth introduced us.

"Nice to meet you." I extended my hand, suppressing
my disquiet with professional ease.

"Yeah, sure," he shrugged. "No worries."

"You argued very intelligently." I dunked an Iced Vo-Vo
biscuit into the Styrofoam cup of scalding tea.

"Brains is what you've gotta use if you've never had an
edge-ja-kay-shun."

"Education just allows you to get into more expensive
trouble," I bantered. "What are you in for? And for how

long?" I continued. Bruce the Tooth grunted and moved away. To a crim, this question is like asking Sir John Kerr if he drinks. Billy Bridges regarded my breach of prison protocol coolly. "Just done a five-year graduation course. Jail, see, is a university where you're sent to figure out ya mistakes and get lectures an' that in better armed-robbery techniques."

I flicked open my notebook and asked him about the changing attitudes to women in male society.

"Get this through your squarehead skull," he said, confiscating my pen. "It's not just blacks and women what get treated like second-class citizens. I bin through years of it too. I know what it's like to be slagged on." Billy had large hands, greedy eyes, and was so top heavy with pectorals I felt sure that if he fell, you'd have to flip him over on his back, like a beetle, before he could get up again. "I can understand why none of youse trust blokes." His voice was low and intense now. "But what I also seen is that youse have never had a real man before, datin' all them boys. Youse have never had anyone who'd stand up to youse. You ain't never had a man make love to ya." Bruce the Tooth beckoned him over to join a group of girls with Sportsgirl cotton tops, nipples turned on to high beam. "I can hack the Women's Movement," he said expansively. "Women are underdogs. Like prisoners. See?"

"Is one of those women your girlfriend?"

"A mate of ours owns a massage parlour. He sends us in the odd freebee."

"Where? How? What about the prison officers?"

"Do you know why fuckin' dog screws hang around in threes? One likes readin', one likes writin', and the other likes hangin' round with intellectuals." His eyes lit up with sly gaiety.

"They're calling you."

He wrapped his fingers around my upper arm. "Rather talk to you, Julia." There was a deceptive languidness to all his movements. "It's the difference between scratching your arse and tearing it." I looked at him, perplexed. "Rough dunny paper's a dime a dozen. You," he sized me up, "are softest Charmin."

Maybe that's why I fell for him. He was such a smooth-talking bastard.

It began with secret calls on the Al Capone (he was teaching me rhyming slang), then smuggled, uncensored letters called "stiffs." He wrote to me about the brutal boys' homes, the police bashings with baseball bats on the balls of the feet where you couldn't see the bruising, the razor blades planted in the soap so blokes would slash themselves in the shower. He'd even eaten nails because hospital was some respite from the prison floggings. Attraction is mysterious, but I know now that it had something to do with the fact that Billy's upbringing, unlike my own, had been a harsh apprenticeship of hatred. I wanted to take his pain away. That's how I saw myself, a human tube of first-aid cream.

After the letters, we graduated to private meetings, faces pressed up against the glass partition. I joined the Prisoners Action Group. Through them I organised poetry sessions. These contact visits were conducted in a row of glass cubicles. Billy and I sat on opposite sides of the table. It was like being stuck inside an aquarium.

"I've been thinking about you . . ." I began.

Years of regular meals, early nights, exercise, and no alcohol had had a Peter Pan effect. He did not look his thirty-one years. "Oh well . . . you're only human." He smiled irresistibly. "What did you think of me at first squizz?"

"I'd never met a prisoner before. I expected you to be, well, hairier!" He leant back in his chair; the complicated

148

tatoos on his folded forearms rippled like the coloured markings on some exotic animal. "I thought beneath all that bluff and bravado you'd be a bit of a . . . yobbo. I didn't expect you to be, well, it sounds patronising, but . . . intelligent and sensitive."

"I do impressions." I heard his shoe thud to the floor.

"After encountering Bruce the Tooth, I'm afraid I judged you all too harshly." He stretched his leg out under the table.

"I dunno . . ." Screws patrolled the corridor, peering into each aquarium. "I reckon you'd make a good judge. Like them, you know how to dispense with justice!" he muttered as he slid his toe underneath the elastic of my underpants. It was like being back at school behind the toilet block, or lying underneath your boyfriend on the lounge-room floor in an agony of orgasmic guilt, one eye out for the sweep of your parents' homecoming headlights. As the guard disappeared, Billy rocked forward on his chair and replaced his foot with his fingers. We remained like that, our faces frozen, as I spoke like a push-button tape recorder, about Keats, Craig Raine, Bruce Dawe, Donne. "Shit," he said, "I'm shakin'. I'm like a dog shittin' razor blades." At the end of the "poetry session," he leant back in his chair and with devout delight slowly licked each finger.

That was the day I learned that objectivity in journalism was a myth.

"A crim?" Kerrie stopped trowelling Vegemite onto her toast. "Have you got kangaroos in the top paddock?" She tapped her temple with the butter knife. When Kerrie had broken up with her boyfriend, she'd moved in, along with a trendy trousseau of pot plants, posters, scales, skim milk, rock music, water bed, and diet-inducing signs to stick on the fridge proclaiming that BOILED EGGS ARE BEAUTIFUL.

"Crims," Kerrie concluded through a mouthful of Kibble-wheat, "make a habit of finding things before people lose them, remember?"

Kerrie didn't understand that the politicians and television executives she dated had exactly the same predatory instincts as Billy. The only difference being that Billy didn't have sufficient capital to set up a corporation. "You'll like Billy." I spooned the Earl Grey tea leaves into the pot. "He's witty, intelligent . . ."

She raised her plucked eyebrows sarcastically. "The reason he's spent most of his life behind bars remains a mystery . . ."

The terrace we lived in was a ramshackle affair, complete with harbour view. Well, more of a glimpse, and then only if you stood on the loo and held a mirror out the window. The walls were papered with political posters: EVE WAS FRAMED, NICARAGUA IS SPANISH FOR VIETNAM, WAR IS MEN'S MENSTRUATION ENVY. An Australia flag was draped over the window as a curtain.

"It'll take time, I know that." I positioned my three-legged teacup on the kangaroo-fur coaster. "Prisoners come out in a worse state than when they went in."

"The only reason you're interested in Billy is that it's another *first* for you." Kerrie angrily slathered another slice. "I mean you've done everything else." She paused to scrape the butter residue off her knife onto the lip of the Vegemite jar. "Except bondage. Firsts are getting rarer and rarer these . . ."

"You are *so* wrong, Kerrie."

"What!" Kerrie gasped, intrigued. "You've *done* bondage?" I watched her squirm into perilous stilettos as she fished up beneath her leather skirt to retrieve a shirttail. Kerrie was wrong about our generation. We had led very protected lives. Not from dope and men and kinky positions, but we had been protected from intimacy all our lives. "He needs me," I said.

"Of course." She lacquered her teased hair in gel. "You're his lifeline."

"I'm going to teach him about music and literature," I explained, separating the garbage into piles of biodegradable and plastics. "And about food and theatre and . . ."

"Sounds like you're allowing for everything . . ." she rolled her Burnt Burgundy–lidded eyes, "except what will happen." Late for work as usual, she tottered towards the door. "Step out of line and he'll be massaging your collar-bone." She clenched her fist fiercely. "Or giving you AIDS, erghhh. Even the straights turn Turd Burglar *inside.*"

"If you don't have anything to be passionate about,"—squeezing the Wettex into a ball, I followed Kerrie's trail of crumbs around the kitchen—"you may as well be dead."

"You might be," she growled and slammed the door.

The bonus for working in the prison laundry was a contact visit. I waited next to the mothers with lips like string and the squawking babies. Billy's name and number were called. I stood up. But it was Bruce the Tooth who appeared, swaggering across the ragged grass. He hurled himself in a neat dive onto the patch of bindi-eyes at my feet.

"Where's Billy?"

"Did his block in the weight yard." His gold eyetooth seemed to be flashing Morse signals at me. "Got three days in the pound. Siddown," he said. "Ya know he's done his nuts over you." I drew my legs demurely beneath me. "Yeah, you've really got him gallopin' the lizard. Been wankin' himself to death, poor bastard." He leant up close to my face. "He's doin' it hard. If he bolts, its gunna be your fault, missy. Look, why don'tcha just let him slap ya with his love-slug now. Once he's filled ya up with billy dunk, it'll all be over. I seen it before." His breath was like the stale water in a vase. "It's not the cunt, it's the hunt. See?" He was muscle-bound and missing one front tooth. "Next debatin' day why don'tcha just slip backstage to the dunnies. We'll create a distraction for the fuckin' dog screws an' you can whack up for him. No skin off of your nose. Look," he said reasonably, "three years without a woman . . . He'll do his lolly before he even gets it in. The sparrows will fly out of his arse. Then you can piss off and let him do his time in peace. . . ." I stood up to go. "Don't come your coy routine with me." He seized my arm. "Youse snobby chicks have seen more ceilings than Michelangelo."

"Women don't count ceiling cracks anymore." I was full of venom by now. "We've had something called the Women's Movement while you've been inside. You know," I said sarcastically, "feminism?" I was on my feet and moving off.

"You middle-class chicks. You make a man eat a mile of your shit just to kiss your arse," he called out after me, tooth flashing. All niggling doubts dissolved that day. I was now determined to transform Billy into a Born-Again Human Being.

During the six months I waited for him, mysterious deliveries appeared on our doorstep. A carton of biscuits. A container filled with cans of Three-Bean Mix. Preloved televisions and car radios. We got used to the anonymous gifts. Every evening after work, I would round the corner of our street in Darlo with Christmas-morning anticipation. I was dazzled by Billy's daring.

"I'm not having all this contraband in the house," Kerrie said, threading herself into a pair of coloured, factory-seconds pantyhose.

"How do you know it's all hot?" I retorted. "Just 'cause he's in jail doesn't mean he's a real criminal. A conviction doesn't always mean a crime, Kerrie."

"Oh, right. Of course. He's just a victim of circumstance with a circumstance of victims."

"Billy said his friends on the outside would look after us."

"That's another thing. I don't like the underworld having our address."

"Faulty pantyhose is hardly underworld. Anyway, you'd better get used to it. He's going to need a place to stay," I hazarded, "when he gets out next year." Kerry shot me a look of pure malice.

"He's not living in this house. And that's that."

"Why?"

Kerrie rolled the pantyhose up her legs. The ventilated crutch was skewwhiff and the waistband reached up under her armpits. "Because a bloke moving in will ruin our fucking rapport!!!"

Later that night we received our final and unscheduled delivery. I was dozing in bed when a hand went over my mouth. How I had fantasised this moment. The curve of each caress. How he would separate me from my clothing with philatelic precision. His vocarious rapture for each basketball scar and birthmark. How his face would distort during lovemaking. How he would call out my name . . . "You're bewdiful," he said, kissing me hard on the mouth. "But babe, to be honest, the most bewdiful thing in the world to me right now would be a steak."

After a contact visit, Billy had just walked out of jail. He had simply taken the place of one of his younger brothers. They had exchanged clothes, heads had been counted, and Billy, surrounded by a cluster of visitors, had walked out free. When discovered, his imposter would get six months for public mischief. And now Billy owed his brother one. That was how it worked in their world. Billy's plan was to "stay snookered" at my place until we could organise a car and some Bugs Bunny. "Money?" I hazarded a guess. Then

we would do the Harold Holt—"Bolt" he decoded for me—
up to Joh country.

I was a journalist. I knew the penalties for aiding a fugitive from justice. But causes were my cause. To me, it was the jails that were immoral and incarceration the crime.

We washed down the meal with Germaine Greers and Donald Ducked on the Rory O'Moore.

By morning, Billy had fixed everything. The fridge door now closed without the aid of a hockey strap. The table no longer listed. The ironing board, rusted into a state of rigor mortis, was now oiled and put away.

"I knew he'd change every . . . ergh," Kerrie gagged. She had put coffee in the teapot. "Why can't he be inept like other men?" She got the ironing board back out of the cupboard and snapped it to attention. "First he rearranges our furniture, next it'll be our facial features." Billy was doing chin lifts on the kitchen doorframe. "You can't stay here."

"Are you wearing that dress for a bet or what?" Billy tweaked the hem of Kerrie's vinyl miniskirt as she sidled past him sullenly to have another go at making a cup of tea. On the counter were the remnants of a dope deal, some hash, and a half-eaten Mars bar. Kerrie dumped them unceremoniously in the garbage bin.

"It's flirting with fate to have contraband in the house."

"I like flirting." Billy talked like that. In jail you trade on your repartee. It's a currency.

"Dope causes cancer," she said, wiping coffee off her skirt with a Wettex. "I steer clear of Mars bars, monosodium glutamate, alcohol, peanut butter, bongs, salt, and too much sex."

Billy thudded softly back to earth. "Why live?" He retrieved the Mars bar from the bin and ate it in one gluttonous mouthful. He sniffed under his arms. "God, a bit whiffy under the old warwicks." Kerrie looked at me. "Warwick farm, arm," I deciphered. Then he swigged a gulp of milk from the carton. "Ergh . . . got any flavouring? Can't drink it raw. The nipple's still in it."

Kerrie seized the carton from his hands. "Oh, I'm sorry we're not satisfying our guest from Her Majesty's Parramatta Hilton." She thrust it back into the fridge and strode past him with exaggerated indifference.

"Youse middle-class babes have a few misconceptions about our legal system." He wrapped his fingers tightly around her wrists, right where a pair of handcuffs go. "Basically everything depends on a group of twelve people of average ignorance, chosen to decide who has the best lawyer. Kerrie's Kangaroo Court," he said affably, "can I appeal against me conviction, Your Honour?"

Kerrie went red in the face. It was a meltdown. Crims have this effect on women. The Prisoners Action Group was made up of females: teachers, journos, socialites, social workers, writers, film stars, even a famous senator. I attribute it now to the Ned Kelly Complex, the knight in rusty armour. But I didn't know that then. "Maybe . . ." she bantered, not fighting his grip. "I'll *try* anyone once."

"And I'm used to penal servitude." He lifted the lids on his acid-blue eyes. Kerrie stood still, caught out.

That was when I told Kerrie I agreed with her. It was time Billy and I headed north. Having a man round the house was ruining our fucking rapport.

Being on the run was like being in a B-grade gangster movie. What's more, the car Billy had chosen was a huge, shiny Chevy, complete with tail fins and whitewall tyres. It was large enough for us to swim laps in the backseat. He drove fast, leaving a pedestrian purée up and down the median strip. By the time we crossed the border, the vinyl seats were slippery with our sweat.

We southerners call Queensland the Deep North. All of Australia retires to the Gold Coast, to identical apartment blocks called "Xanadu Towers" and "Shangrila Chevron." Calculatedly thin bodies clad in lurid, frivolous teenage fashions swivel to reveal antediluvian heads. Queensland boasts the highest divorce rate, the highest alcohol consumption, the highest number of repossessions, and consumes more tranquillisers than any other state. Crocodiles have a habit of dining on humans. Wives cut off the appendages of unfaithful husbands. Politicians own racehorses. Aborigines hang themselves in their cells with mysterious regularity. Street marches are banned, abortions are illegal, and homosexuals are imprisoned.

Apart from that, it is Paradise.

We dumped the car with an ex-con at the border and waited for Leon. "A lawyer mate," Billy said. "Cool. Leon does a good job for the Prisoners Action Group. He likes the boys and a bit of rough trade." His, I was told, was a "safe house."

He arrived in a decapitated V-Dub. "Go topless. Rent a convertible" was scrawled in candy pink down the side of the duco. Leon was weedy, bow-legged, sported the residue of teenage acne, and had trouble getting people to remember to put his name on their Christmas card list. He was displeased to discover that Billy had a human handbag in his luggage. He put me in the back with the bags, where he obviously felt I belonged. His voice was distorted in the wind, so I only caught every second word about his current cases and the battles he and the Queensland Prisoners Action Group were waging against the infamous Bogga Road jail.

We ate lunch in Froggies and Woggies BYO French restaurant. Halfway through the entrée, Leon informed me that I was a wanker. "The things you're working for just split the movement's solidarity." His tone was one of thinly disguised contempt.

"Come on! The extension of superficial amenities to prisoners has not given the prison population . . ." I grimaced as Billy belted the bottom of the tomato sauce bottle and wiped the globules over his garlic prawns, "less compelling reasons to fight. . . . Don't eat off your knife my darling."

"Our lovemaking has ruined me," Billy beamed. "Billy Bridges, the man Katingal, Grafton, Bogga Road couldn't break. Undone by a mere woman!" He planted a prawny and proprietorial kiss on my mouth. "Once, me and Bruce the Tooth, we intimidated this screw, see . . ."

"Bruce and I," I corrected automatically, impatient to continue my debate with Leon.

". . . got this bar heater off of him, pinched an aluminum pie dish from the officers' mess and two pieces of T-bone from their kitchen. Took about two bloody hours to grill it, but babe, what a bloat-out, but."

"Billy, you shouldn't end a sentence with a preposition."

"Okay, I'll end it with a proposition." Hidden by the tablecloth, he slid his hand between my thighs. "You wanna hit the Roberta?"

Roberta Flack, sack, I decoded and crossed my legs. Retrieving his mangled hand, he continued his meal. "You honestly think, Leon, that a few superficial concessions will result in the prisoners losing . . . Billy, do you *have* to eat with your fingers? . . . the unity of hunger and discomfort?"

"Why do we have to talk about the fuckin' jail all the fuckin' time?" Billy slammed down his fork and hurled himself back into the plush red-velvet booth. "Julia, I don't want you goin' to the debates no more. It's a jungle in there. Debatin' days was only good for their rort value. All them mind-game-crim-capers. Sure, we mouthed off about corruption, but it was you babes we wanted to corrupt!" Billy flung himself up from the table and announced that he was off to shake hands with the unemployed. A tepid smile pinched the corners of Leon's lips.

As soon as Billy had disappeared into the men's toilets, Leon fished a pickle out of the jar with his fingers, crunched it between his yellow teeth, then offered the other half to me. "How long do you think physical attraction can last?" He didn't wait for my reply. "Week? Ten Days?" It was only after I'd bitten into the gherkin that I noticed the cold sore in the crease of his lips. "Masturbation's no big deal inside. Just like taking a piss, apparently. Plastic wrapper from a Drum packet is best. You've just got to smear a ton of margarine round the inside. Or they get a bum chum and go drilling for Vegemite. Some of the guys inside are double adaptors, but most become Hocks. Hocks give it. And Cats take it," he pronounced in a half-mocking tone. "You did know that, didn't you?"

Billy slid back into the booth and placed his warm hands round my throat. I jumped. "I brung you this." A gold chain slithered down the front of my shirt. "Take a butchers. It's clean," he emphasised. "I just made the bloke an offer he couldn't knock back."

"What?" I jolted away from him. "To break both his legs?"

"If you promise that you're through with all that jail-reform stuff, I'll steer clear of all me old crim mates. Otherwise," he brooded, "we'd better call it quits. . . . So, what is it? Chinas?"

"China plates," I shook his hand, "mates," and sealed the deal with a kiss. Leon, disdainful, began a close study of the ashtray.

"God, you've ruined me forever, you foxy lady. And anyway," Billy came up for air, "you *can* end a sentence with a *but*, 'cause," he smirked victoriously, "*but* is a conjunction . . . but!"

After lunch, Leon drove us to Brisbane to visit Billy's parents. They lived in a suburban bungalow which Billy called the "Fibro Majestic." A ceramic Mexican, complete with cactus, lounged against the electronic doorbell. The crew-cut lawn was adorned with statues of stunted aborigines, spears poised. A brass plaque above the door christened the house "Robjune." It was the whole kitsch catastrophe.

Robb Bridges opened the door to his son. He glared at me suspiciously. "Happy Oyster," he said fiercely. I looked at Billy, bewildered. He shook hands with his father.

"Happy Easter to you too, Pop. Where's the cook?"

Billy's mother, June, was holding court out the back by the keg. The family were as thick as what they were— thieves. Billy's father grunted at my rounded vowels and moved away. Australia is not a classless society. But although, as in England, the Born to Rule right-wingers may feel themselves to be superior, nobody here feels inferior. Billy's father dredged up some phlegm and, eyeing me coldly, hawked into the garden.

"You're not one of them *feminists*, is ya?" Billy's mum scrutinised me. "Like Ger-maine Greer. Sittin' round talkin' about their . . ." she glanced about to ensure the exclusivity of our conversation," . . . vageenas." June lowered her amplitudinous body into the banana chair and motioned for me to sit beside her. "I brung me boys up good. They're not real burg-u-lars. They're dark sheep, that's all. Ya know," she said conspiratorially, "black horses. Billy's gunna git somewhere in this world but. Not like his *f*-ing father." Her face darkened. "He don't look ya in the eye when he talks to ya, ya know?" She squinted into my face. "His father would steal the milk out of his grandmother's tea."

Billy's father was scrutinising me for the slightest trace of distaste at the crocheted dolls' dresses covering the toilet rolls or the painting of the street urchin trickling pastel tears.

Mrs. Bridges sighed despondently, then cheered up in a

flash. "I like him goin' with a better-educated girl and that. You can act as a bit of a, you know . . . detergent. From crime and that." She beamed at me. "You could learn him a lot."

"What's wrong babe?" Billy said protectively. "Has someone insulted you?" He flexed every muscle, so that his torso looked even more like an ice-cream cone. "Has someone hurt ya?" Billy's cousin was a car dealer. He had given him an old Dodge and we were driving it back to Surfers' Paradise through Florida and Miami, migratory suburbs, flown south to escape the American winter.

"Were you a Hock," I gulped, "inside?"

"Why? What's Leon been saying to you? Don't worry about him. He's weak as a railway cuppa. Couldn't spread marg on a Sao."

Relieved, I reported that his parents were good salt-of-the-earth types. Basic. Billy's body tensed. "Don't patronise me," he hissed. "I've bin a specimen all me life. Cat psychologists and social workers, pokin' and proddin' me. 'Oh . . . he's bright.'" he mimicked, "'How amazin'. And his father works in an iron foundry.' There's only one good thing about the workin' class," he swerved to avoid a squashed wombat, "and that's gettin' out of it."

Making love that night he bit my lip too hard, till it bled.

Being in love with a man in jail is like being in love with a priest. A no-risk romance. Cloistered in the confessional of the Contact Room, you present censored versions of yourselves, passions telescoped by the pressure of frustration. It was only now that I began to realise how little I knew about Billy Bridges. I don't know how long I stayed with him on the Gold Coast. The days and nights blurred into each other through a haze of heat and confusion.

At first, I dismissed the tension between us as a symptom of jail withdrawal. Time, I'd always rationalised, was to stop everything from happening at once. But time was something Billy didn't wait for. Drink, dance, rage, pull bongs, screw, eat, drive fast, make money, drink . . . for weeks we did it all at once.

Then I blamed the prison hierarchy. Inside, Billy had been King Pin. Outside, he was a nobody. Our pact had exiled him to a limbo land between the criminal and white-collar worlds. I gave him a cultural tourist visa and took him to concerts, the opera, the art gallery. But he was ill at ease, convinced everybody was looking at him. At the beach, I slathered his anaemic muscles in sun-screener. Billy didn't really have a great Aussie tan; it was more a billiard-ball white. Not only that, he couldn't swim. He looked conspicuous and vulnerable on the sand, like something just washed in. And he compensated for his unease by becoming brash. When the surf lifesaver told him to stop playing Frisbee with beer cans, Billy inquired if he liked travel and sex. When the lifesaver, bemused, smiled that, yes he did, Billy wanted to know why then didn't he fuck off? I snapped back at him, and his eyes narrowed to slits of mistrust. Once I shrank from his raised arm. He was only scratching an armpit.

My next excuse was the fact that he'd missed the advent of the Women's Movement. Not in theory, but in practice. Taking boys' homes into account, Billy had been inside for most of his life, which was why he expected me to make the toast and change the toilet roll. Billy thought PMT was the express train from Newcastle.

Jail was also to blame for his bedridden brain. Our sex was frantic, masturbatory. He wanted me to pretend things, that I was a young boy, or to make noises as though it were the first time, and to comply, at the appearance of the Vaseline jar, to what he called an excursion up the Khyber.

When he'd had time to rehabilitate from all these things,

I then blamed our tensions on sunburnt brains. Too much sun sends you troppo north of the border. This explained his muscle-bound "friends" dropping round at midnight to drink Fourex and swap tales of rorts and rampages. It explained him disappearing in hire cars and returning drunk or drugged. It explained his insistence on frantic exercise, jogging in the equatorial sun, up the highway, down the stormwater drain, urging me on when I felt nauseous with the heat, then tackling me down in the lantana and wrenching the leg of my shorts to one side. It explained why I felt frightened.

And yet, still I refused to believe that my feelings for him were fraudulent.

We pulled up outside a marshmallow-pink mansion in Surfers' Paradise. The manmade canals seemed to breed speedboats that buzzed up and down continuously till dusk. Billy homed in on the beer-gutted billionaires by the far side of the pool. Though grunting illiterates, they all spoke fluent Tax Evasion.

The women, marooned by the pretzels, were clad in gaudy lamé dresses and sequin-studded ensembles. Lips, teeth, eyes, thighs, every bit of them glittered as they raised their talons, ready to sink into a high-rise developer divorcé. In brassy affected voices they spoke passionately to me about the merits of wallpapering a dining room Moroccan cream.

I slipped my arm through Billy's. "It's prehistoric. Men and women at different sides of a party. You'd think you were all gay the way you cluster together."

The men eyed me up and down as if I were a housing prospect. *"Banned!* We don't have homos or bisexuals in Queensland," Bazza the Real Estate entrepreneur boasted. "This is a family state."

"Here you are, love." Prawnhead, a dentist-cum-oyster-farmer, offered me something from his plate. "Wrap your laughing gear around that lot." They all watched me swallow the oyster.

"Cripes," a National party politician called Porky said to Billy, "she didn't get that mouth sucking strawberries." The men guffawed. On the pretext of assassinating a mozzie, Billy jerked his arm out of mine.

"Did you know that oysters are bisexual?" I said matter-of-factly. "You'll have to arrest Prawnhead's oyster leases under the Family Law and Decency Act." The live band was playing Muzak: dull cover versions of the latest hits. The chandeliers hanging incongruously from the canvas roof of the marquee shed a garish light on my companions. They were drinking with exaggerated gusto, attempting to mask their confusion at the notion that they'd been eating poofters.

Billy ordered me a cab. He said he had to talk business. "Porky's got a few propositions."

I knew that any propositions made by these men would end in a sentence. "Do you want to go back inside?"

"Runnin' a bit short, aren't I, of sausage and mash."

"So? I've got plenty of cash . . ."

"Every time we go into a fuckin' shop, or down the fuckin' pub, *you're* payin'. How do you reckon that makes me feel? Everyone looks at me like I'm a weak bastard. There's no way me old man would've let me mum pay for nothin'. I've had a gut full. Look love, I don't wanna be a shitman forever." He steered me out of earshot of the cabbie. "I could just do one job to get us set up an' that. Then I could look after ya . . ."

"What about our pact?"

"Besides," he said, "I've hit the Johnny Rapers in Steak 'n Kidney. They'll be lookin' up here soon. I've gotta get on the right payroll. It's best you shoot through," he said with

163

feigned cheerfulness. "You're about as popular round here as a fart in a space suit!"

The next morning I was up early and went with Leon out to Bogga Road jail. The car radio warned we were heading for a heat wave.

Billy was waiting in the hallway for me when I got back. "Some guy's bin puttin' work on you." His face wore a predatory expression. "A guy I used to share a yard with's cellmate's brother seen you at Bogga Road talkin' to Jimmy the Toecutter."

"Talking, yes." I was panic-stricken for a moment and wriggled past him. "Not all men talk with their crutch."

"He'd charm the pants off of his own grandmother."

"What guy you used to share a yard with?" I crossed into the kitchen. "You promised not to see any of your old crim mates." The steaks hadn't been thawed. I ran them under scalding water.

"It's okay, babe." He exhaled a blast of brandy and bong breath. "I've hung up me gloves." He kneaded my breast. "It's just that it's dangerous goin' into jails. Psychologically, as well as friggin' physically. Not to mention your reputation." He tugged down on my fly. "I've already defended your honour today, twice. The boys reckon you're slumming it, that you're just usin' me."

I sliced into an onion. "I can't just toss it in! There are submissions to be made for the women back at Mulawah, play rehearsals, poetry readings . . ." It was still 104 degrees. The house itself sweated in the heat. Even lifting the knife was too burdensome.

"Let's stay in bed for three weeks straight." He bit my earlobe. "Bin shakin' hands with Mrs. Palmer and her five daughters for fifty-eight months straight." He wrenched at my jeans. "Up until I bolted to be with you, the only stimulation the old boy got was the odd dip in crab emulsion." He pushed me up against the fridge door.

"Billy," my voice faltered, "you're cunt struck!"

His eyes went dark. He turned and leant on the sink, breathing deeply. "Look babe, what with me boyish looks and charms, I ain't never had trouble findin' a bedmate." He forced a smile. "Weak in the pants I am. But you're my woman now." He lunged and began to caress me but I recoiled.

"I'm *not* your woman. I'm not anybody's woman. Look, Billy. I think it's time I went back to Sydney. I'm on committees. I've got professional commitments. Deadlines. And I've neglected my friends . . ."

"Ask them to come up. Leon won't mind . . ."

"I like to have my own friends."

His affected affability dissolved. "Embarrassed of me, aren't ya? In front of your friends. Your Deep Water Front Socialists. 'Cause I can't make jokes about herpes and holistic healing and inter-fucking-facing." He hurled me up against the back door. "You're trainin' me to become your human handbag that you can take on your arm to premieres and dinner parties. You're just like them middle-class housewives frontin' Prisoners Aid Meetings 'cause it makes 'em horny. Are you horny? I could make you really slum it." He was grinding me into the door. "Like a few bruises? You can wear 'em like trophies. Tell everyone about your animal. Licks his bitch all over." He grabbed the knife off the cutting board. "Whose bitch are you?" He pressed the cool gleaming blade against my larynx. "Whose bitch are you?"

From somewhere far away I heard my own voice, pale with terror. "Billy's," it said.

I was still huddled out on the back verandah when I heard Leon arrive home. His wheedling voice drifted out across the boards. "Oh yes. I know her type. They pontificate that 'sex is a lubricant of the consumer society,' but why do you think they become obsessed with crims? They want to be dominated. Thrown across a bed and ravaged. A bit of

rough trade. It's the latest fad for middle-class, well-edu-
cated women. Scum can be fun." His laughter rose to a
lilting shrill.

I slumped against the rail, overcome by my own insin-
cerity. A good middle-class girl, I *was* secretly horrified by
the way Billy ate, and irritated when he put his running
shoes in the fridge to cool them off.

"How will Bruce the Tooth react, eh? He gets out
soon. . . . Beer?" I heard the hiss of a ring-pull can. "And he'll
be straight up here after you. He'll squash her, like a cockroach. Squelch."

"What the fuck are you insinuatin'?"

"Look. I know you were on with Bruce."

"The Tooth and me were fuckin' mates. You fuckin'
queer. You're the fuckin' Cat. Don't lay your shit on me!"

"Bruce told me you were his boy."

What I had mistaken for strength in Billy was nothing
more than nerves and bravado. What I had mistaken for love
was nothing but a love of his own bleak notoriety. Our
Idealogically Sound commitment was nothing more than a
Mills and Boon romance. After all the effort I'd put into
changing him, I could now only complain that he wasn't the
man he was when I first met him.

In bed that night he was manic. He pushed my head
down into his lap. These things did not happen to me. I was
a B grade journalist. A University graduate. I was studying
law part-time. . . . He wouldn't let me come up for air. I was
getting RSI of the mouth. I had a St. George Building Society
account. Drove a Honda Civic . . . He was insisting that I
must never leave him. That he was *lost without me.* I was an
NRMA subscriber. A paid-up member of the Labor party.
I wrote articles on the Changing Face of Feminism. . . . He
said he'd been betrayed that much, he'd become *sus of everyone.* "But I thought I seen loyalty and honesty in you." I was

famous back in Sydney for holding forth over morning muesli (unsweetened) about feelings being transitory, that it was beliefs which mattered. In the still air, he cried into my hair that I was *his woman,* that *no other bastard would ever have me now.* He would kill, he said, to keep me. I had the Mozart operas on compact disc and could jack up a car. I was capable. Energetic. Efficient. I would confront him, talk reason, and stand my ground.

The next day when he was out jogging, I filled my pockets with coins. Embarrassed in case he didn't hand over enough change, Billy only paid with big notes. His pockets were bulging with Kembla Grange. I raided them now, booked a flight, called a cab, and fled.

Back in Sydney I sat in the lounge room of our Darlinghurst terrace feeling numb. Kerrie was whingeing. She'd slept with a friend's lover last night after a drunken party and was filled with remorse. "He wasn't even a good fuck," she concluded, dropping Beroccas into a glass. "Didn't even touch the sides." And on top of that, her water bed had sprung a leak portside. Soula had been home to visit her parents. They had now arranged for her to marry Stavro. "He's really off. He's got a huge space between his teeth and this really hairy back." Debbie had lost her surfing heat and had dropped round for some sympathy.

No fuss was made about my return. Kerrie said she hoped next time I wanted an off-beat record collection, that I'd go for classical, not criminal. And then they simply assigned Billy to the bottom of the linen press, along with the scuba, abseiling, photography, pottery, spray cans, and screen-printing paraphernalia.

"I mean, she who hesitates is celibate, right?" Kerrie puffed herself up with self-justification, then just as suddenly sagged. "What am I going to do? No point asking you, ya goody-two-shoes. You're always in control. Nothing shitty ever happens to you."

"No," I said. "Nothing." I was the sort of person a girl-friend rang at midnight when a boyfriend had left her for Another Man. I was the sort of person they rang for the phone number of Legal Aid, marriage counsellors, the AIDS Hotline. I knew what minister held the portfolio for Veterans' Affairs. I'd held the hands of mates in preterm abortion clinics and acted as "support person" for all the single mothers in our circle—forehead mopping, back rubbing, and breathing encouragement.

Upstairs, I lay in bed, alert to every creak and groan in the house. I felt his presence in the fabric of the air. For the first time I knew where to lay the blame. I, not he, had been the con artist. Emotional break-and-enter. White-collar crime of the heart. I shivered and curled up against the wall. The streetlight filtering through the venetian blinds lay like bars across my bed.

A Melanoma Called Bruce

I drove my bomb of a V-Dub down Kurnell Road, Cronulla, at dawn, past the stinking rubbish tip, past the Leagues Club, home of the Sharks, past the factories and the smouldering rubber tyres and burnt-out car bombs. This was Captain Cook's landing place. "The birthplace of our nation," we'd learnt at school.

Cronulla was in a time warp of flanno shirts, desert boots, and panel vans. It was still a full-on surf city. Nothing had changed since my days as a Surfin Gherkin.

There are heaps of gangs in Sydney. There's the Head-bangers, Footyheads, Bull Dykes, Petrol and Revheads, the Hubcap Biters, Vegie-brains, Wogs, Dapto Dogs or Chocolate Frogs, and, even lower on the racist rung, the Slope-heads, who are hated 'cause they're head-and-a-halfs. We Skips and Joeys used to pay out on the Wogs for taking all the jobs, now the Wogs blame the Asian Invasion. There are heaps more gangs—the Bong-Brains, Cone Heads, Mods, Trogs, Rude Boys, Rock-a-Billys, Westies . . . But hottest of all are the Waxheads. Surfers are an amphibious, beach-

169

dwelling species, who hunt in packs for females with "margarine legs." You know, easily spread. Chicks are nicknamed bush pigs, swamp hogs, maggots, spitters, or swallowers.

I hadn't surfed at Cronulla for untolds. Five years in fact. Not since the day I spun them out by taking my brother's board out. Couldn't stand up or anything. I just grovelled, wobbling in the shallow white water. The boys in my Greenhill gang told me I was a scumbag moll and to fuck off out of their territory. I got dropped. Bruce spat on my back and drove over my board in his Combi. He started going round with Tracey after that, before she went full-on footy head. Then ever since I'd left home I'd been surfing up the Northern beaches. I'd turned into a bit of a contest-head too. Only amateur . . . But I knew I'd never be hot until I got a bit of recognition from the boys at Cronulla. That was why I'd come back. Revenge and a bit of recco.

The waves would be working at Voodoo. I trekked through the sand hills where we used to come after dark to pull bongs and make cracker night noises at the lights of the oil refinery. The sun was rising over a solid south swell. It was six-to-eight-foot perfection with a light offshore. I stood in the parking lot, watching the sets build. The lines were jacking up with the tide and pounding the reef. Voodoo is heaps dangerous. Not just 'cause of the hozzos, you know, the waves that hospitalise you, but they'd also whacked the sewerage plant there. How else would you mark the birthplace of the nation?

But the only sharks hanging there this morning were the two-legged kind. A station wagon was pulled up on the lip of the car park overlooking the reefs. The guys inside were either asleep in the back or pulling a morning bong before getting out there for an Early. I pulled on my fluoro vest. This was their territory. I'd have to get in a few waves before they got out there.

By the time the boys surfaced in their sluggoes, I was waxed up and doing warmup exercises. In their multicoloured wetties, they looked like Licorice Allsorts. Sussing them out, I nearly peaked. It was Bruce and his mates.

"Perf surf." Squid hawked and spat a projectile globule of phlegm onto the car-park asphalt.

"*Filthy* waves," agreed Bodge. "Classic." He looked spastic with the rubber arms of his wettie dangling beside his body. He was a classic Surf Nazi—the type of guy whose party trick is to get drunk and set his pubic hairs alight.

"Whoa! I'm *out* there!" Bruce scrunched his Poppa orange-juice carton and sent it rattling into the garbage bin.

Board tucked neatly under my arm, I jogged past them towards the sea. "Whoa!" added Bodge, his eyes burning holes in my Speedo-clad buttocks. "I'm *in* there."

"Shit! Surf chickens." Squid punctuated his sneer with another guttural gurgling.

Looking at those gaping left tubes as they crashed into the Voodoo reef, I got nervous and paddled into the lineup too early. With no one else out there it's really hard to judge where the sets are peaking. I sat astride my board. The sun was rising and I strained to see through the glare. The horizon lifted. I was too far inside. Right smack bang in the impact zone.

"She won't hack it," I heard Bruce reassure his mates as they paddled out behind me. "Chicks can't surf. It's their tits. Puts 'em off balance." The three mates, known locally as the Bob Hawke Surf Team (they work as brickie's labourers in the winter and live on the dole all summer), grunted in agreement. Girl surfers were only tolerated because of their perv value—the guys paddle out behind and watch them duck dive.

As the wave approached, I flicked the Speedo elastic over my chickers, built up speed, then hoisted myself up on my arms and sunk my shin into the tail as the whole board submerged. The sea went into a spin rinse.

Craning over my shoulder, I saw the boys bob up after the wall of water had washed over their heads. I'd beaten them out the back. They'd be spewing.

They made their way into the takeoff zone. Sitting astride their thrusters, surveying the swells, Bruce, Bodge, and Squid gave me the full-on hairy eyeball.

"Dum-dum-dum-dum-dum." Knifing the air with a flattened palm, Bodge warbled the theme song of *Jaws.*

"Well, check out who it is!" Bruce planted his hands on his hips. "We heard you'd turned into a full-on Av cat, Deb." There had always been aggro between Cronullites and the seaweed-munchers from Avalon. "You can't surf Voo-ie, little girl," he scoffed. "You'll get killed!"

Sitting on the inside, I could see a set peaking. Knowing my backhand was hot, I was relishing pulling into one, I lay down and started stroking towards the wave. Bruce started paddling for the same one. "This is a *man's* wave!" he yelled. But I was certain he wouldn't drop in on me. Not on the first wave of the day.

I felt the swell pick me up. Hoisting myself up as it peaked, I was jacked heavily and took a vertical drop. Out of the corner of my eye, I could see Bruce taking off. The bastard. I dropped low, put my weight on my back foot, and swept into a heavy backhand bottom turn. That Neanderthal nerd had delayed his first turn. Caught behind the section, I was crushed by the lip. Chundered. Dunked. The Human Teabag. Surfacing asthmatically, I squirmed back onto my board and paddled out of the impact zone, cursing this shark-fucker. Back in the lineup, the boys smirked and sniggered. They yahooed Bruce as he paddled out to join them. I sat outside waiting for the next set, feeling piss-weak.

As surfie chicks, we had folded their towels, bought their Chicko Rolls, minded their milkshakes, turtle-backed ("Once you're on your back," the boys told us, "you're fucked"), and got branded. We used to cut our boyfriends' names out in paper and sticky-tape them onto our tummies to get a tan tattoo. Most of my friends would have a bulk dossier branded on their bellies by the end of every summer. Trace had the most, but that was before she went full-on footy head. If I ever get cancer the malignant growths will be in the shape of only one name. Imagine it, a melanoma called Bruce. But, that's why I'd come back here wasn't it? To get a Bruce-ectomy.

A heavy lull set in. Frustrated, I paddled for some that which didn't break. To beat the tedium, the boys tried to stand up on their boards and balance in the still water. Arms semaphoring, they chucked three-sixties. Bruce pulled his board down into the water, took aim, and let it fly at me like a harpoon. I wasn't worried. Board-flicking was a big Lull Practice. His leg rope stopped it just short of my head. I reckon the reason I hate house pets is 'cause, as a teenager, I went out with so many animals . . .

Two other guys were paddling out. I recognised Garry. At school he'd been this full-on aggro animal. Now he was a chalkie. The guy with him was a wind surfer from Avalon. A total trendoid with an E-type haircut—curly on top and shaved round the sides.

"Whatcha doin' hangin' round with an Av cat pineapple head, Gazza?" Bruce droned in disgust.

"What happened to the surf?" whinged Garry. "Triple J reckoned it was glassy, four-to-five-foot perfection. This is . . . ah . . . Damien."

"Aren't you a wind wanker, mate?" Bruce interrogated, hostile as buggery.

"Hey Deb!" Garry grinned and started to paddle towards

me. "Ripper. How goes it? Gettin' many? Haven't seen you round for heaps."

"It's chocker enough out here without chicks," Bruce growled. "Dunno what the world's coming to. Chicks surfin' up and down the coast. Spokespersons and chairpersons an' all that *shit.*"

"Yeah," chorused Squid. "And what the fuck are they gunna call mailmen?" he yelled over at me. "Person persons?"

"Yeah, I reckon." Garry turned tail quickly and paddled back to them. Surfers' emotions are kind of ingrown. On their lonesomes they're not total rejects. It's only in packs that they turn into walking, talking life-support systems to a wetsuit.

The surf had gone flat as a tack. We all sat astride our boards waiting and watching for the sets. Nervous, I played noughts and crosses with my nail in the board wax while the boys talked.

"I dunno," Damien said, checking me out. "I reckon feminism's let us blokes sort of tap into our own sensitivity." He fished down his Okanuis to rearrange his balls. "Feminism's made me heaps more sensitive and vulnerable."

The Bob Hawke Surf team swapped looks of loathing. "S'pose your shit's stopped stinkin' too." Squid took aim with a missile of mucous. It slithered down the nose of Damien's board.

"In fact," Damien continued unperturbed, directing his comments at me, "I now consider myself a male feminist."

"What does that make you? A closet lesbian . . . Shit!" Squid heaved his board sideways to avoid a nasty-looking clump of toilet paper and turd. "Blind mullets," he warned and the boys lifted up their legs.

"It's a spin out, I know. I mean the prospect of the compulsory orgasm freaks me right out too guys."

Bodge looked at him blankly. "Speak Australian, wouldja?"

"Women," Damien elaborated, "are demanding more in bed these days."

Bruce shrugged. "Are they?" Squid peeled off some board wax and moulded it into a pellet.

I swung my legs up onto the board to avoid a floating condom. It drifted over against Bruce's leg. I saw him scoop it up on the sly and fill it with sea water.

"I'm not bullshittin' you. Women are changing heaps. They expect heaps more. These days, if ya wanna swing in on a girl you've gotta crap on about recipes and PMT and shit like that."

"Fuckin' Jesus," Bruce moaned. "Whatever happened to the good, old-fashioned romantic days when you could just ask a chick for a fuck?"

"Yeah," the boys rejoined. "Bloody oath."

Damien paddled over towards me. "You cop a lot of flack being a sensitive male," he lamented.

I looked away. Living in the city I'd met heaps of Damiens. It didn't take long to sus that men only called themselves feminists in the hope of getting a more intelligent fuck.

"You reckon it's easy being an animal?" Bruce jammed his board between Damien and me.

"Yeah!" Squid was struggling to articulate their intellectual dilemma. "If you don't ask a chick to bed she calls you a chocolate-doughnut hunter."

"And if you do," Garry commiserated, "you're a perverted, psychopathic rapist."

"I don't want you to take this as an insult, fella, seeing as how I've only just met you." Bruce dunked the nose of Damien's board. "But you're a limp turd."

Damien snarled. "Yeah, well, I'd advise you to grow an

extra brain cell, mate." He swiped Bruce's hand into the water. "The one you've got must get so lonely up there." I lay still, all eyes and ears. Bruce flexed every muscle in his six bronzed feet of flesh. "Just a little joke . . ." Damien grovelled. But Bruce peaked. He flicked the condom at Damien. It missed and landed with a thud on Squid's board. Squid torpedoed it back. And it was on. Missiles of seaweed, wax pellets, and the condom bomb exploded all around. Bruce dived off his board, capsizing Damien. "Mate, hang on. I just had me teeth capped . . ." Damien squealed, seconds before he was submerged.

The boys didn't see the set swelling in behind them. I was sitting outside, so I lay down quietly and started to paddle with the back foot, angling farther and farther inside. By the time the boys saw the set and started racing in for it, I was in the prime takeoff pozzie. The biggest set of the morning jacked up. It was eight feet.

"Maggot!" Bruce shrieked across the water at me. "Surf chicken." He flapped his arms. "Buck-buck-buck . . ."

Halfway up the face I swung round. It was a late takeoff. I'd only had to paddle once and I was up on my feet. The face of the wave sucked out vertically. It felt like free falling. I knew I had to keep the rail in, or I'd nose-dive. I rode to the bottom, vertical, sensed the wave's power, and leant into a heavy backhand bottom turn with full power off the back foot.

Glancing down the line out towards the flat I saw the guys hanging over the edge. None of them was in the right position to take off. They'd missed it. I turned under the pitching lip, changed rails, set a line, leant forward in perfect trim, and I was flying. The whole lip cascaded over my head. I was in a huge cavern, feeling the power of the tube. The noise was enormous, deafening, blue. Four or five seconds in a screaming tube feels like forever. I could see the sky, like another world, through the watery membrane. Racing under the edge, I freaked, thinking the liquid cylinder was going to close out. Then instead of pulling out the back of the wave, I decided to race the second section. I back-doored the barrel and raced under the lip as it passed over. Sensing that the wave was going to collapse behind me, I braced myself, accelerated, and went flying out the other side of the section. The tube just spat me out. I went into a full face-to-the-water roundhouse cutback, bounced off the foam, did a couple of turns, and then pulled off into the channel.

A long line of late-risers were watching from the rocks. They whooped and hollered as I emerged from the hozzo. Convinced I'd been chundered, the Bob Hawke Surf Team gawked at me as I paddled out the back. They were blown away.

"She pulled into that hozzo tube."

"Shit! She went off."

"That's hot."

"Classic."

"She killed it."

"Bullshit. You reckoned she couldn't surf."

For the next few waves, all the boys were on their best behaviour. No hassling. No dropping in. They surfed nervously, freaked in case they fell off in front of me.

The wind turned onshore. It blew it out severely. The water was chopped up. We all went in together, the boys keeping a respectful distance behind me. I passed the other guys paddling out. Ocky, Wogo, Midi, Pots, Gobbo, Kong, Rabbit, Gordo, Gibbo, Grub, Zit, Teary, Horse, Rhino, Picko, Whacker. They pulled out of my way. I had recco.

As I tugged on my trackie a P-plated Celica, shuddering with the bass of a Bruce Springsteen tape, cruised down the sandy track. It was chock-a-block with lipsticked chicks. Long blond hair trailing, dolled up to the dinners, they looked like the girls on that tampon ad. Having checked out the surf report they knew it was working at Voodoo and that the hot surfers would have been here since dawn. Leaning on my board, I chucked a cheesy at them. I wanted to tell them to *go for it!* To fire up. Amp to the max. That the whole wide world was just stretched out in front of us. Things had changed! All we had to do was get out there and get into it!

The driver wound down the window. "What a wanker," she spat.

"Think ya can surf, ya bushie." A peroxided head protruded through the sun roof.

"What are ya tryin' to do, swamp hog?" Daddy's Celica circled me like a four-wheeled shark coming in for the kill. "Lick out the boys, ya brownnoser." The car screeched to a stop.

"There are three types of turd." The prettiest one bent down and selected a rock. "Mus*turd*, Cus*turd*..." She hurled it at my head. "And you, you shit. So piss off!" I lifted my board just in time. The rock bounced off the thruster and broke.

"What are ya tryin' to do? Steal our guys? You're ruinin' it for the rest of us."

Stripped off to bikini pants, they proceeded to lacquer their bare breasts in Sun Factor Four, adjust any stray pubic hairs, light cigarettes, compare tans, fight over the copy of *Tracks,* roll a joint ... and then lie back and wait for the boys.

Plutonium in the Porridge

There is a man shortage. All the men are either married or gay. Or married *and* gay. And the rest have a three-grunt vocabulary: "na," "dunno," and "errgh." Apart from the occasional Pommy poet passing through town, there is nobody. Nothing. Zilch.

You and all your female mates are scraping the bottom of the biological barrel. Kerrie has resorted to her boss. He's married, of course. (It's called sleeping your way to the bottom.) Deb has developed a hubcap-biter streak. (She only goes out with a guy for his car, currently an A grade journo with a Maserati.) Soula's desperate to get married and turn into a Human Handbag. Tracey's having Close Encounters of the Grope kind with an entire footy team. Julia is thinking of going lezzo. (You think about it too, but you're just not into tits and clits.) Compared to masturbation or a meat injection, even a Pommy bath-dodger can seem pretty exotic.

There are not enough Poms to go round. When they lob here on a book promotion, or co-production location, or for

BBC documentaries on Down Under, you and your girl-friends share them round. After all, you are the Stick Sisters and this is an R-rated ration. Giggling, you drink gin and tonics and compare Keats poems quoted in the cot and how they exclaimed over the low-tide marks of your tans. There is one rule: Do not fall in love.

It is the height of summer. Julia calls you. "Ro . . . Pom, film director, sexy . . . ish." Her judgement is summary. "Except for the socks and the"—she swallows hard—". . . sandals."

Melvyn is a hearty rogue elephant of a man, with a beard, crinkly eyes, a pipe, and leather-patched elbows. He tells you he is distantly related to Captain Cook. He calls you darling. My love. My dear. He tells you that you're very beautiful and on the side of the angels. He tells you that if you and he lived in Roman times, you'd go along to the temple of a goddess to give thanks. "Probably to Diana of the Ephesians, the goddess for whom St. Paul declared his hatred in the New Testament, because she liked lovers." He organises a Graham Greene–like dead-letter drop. It is a nineteenth-century courtship. You imagine your love letters going for a vast amount at a London auction. You correspond with pen instead of word processor. Tractor-fed computer A4 just wouldn't look as good beneath glass at the Victoria and Albert.

"I'm going to England. Do my back, would ja?"

Your friends swap censorious glances behind their Polaroids.

"Ro, how can you seriously consider living in a country whose sole contribution to the cuisine of the world is a cucumber sandwich?" Julia pummels the sand into a pillow and spreads her towel, then herself, onto this makeshift mattress. "Make Melvyn come here."

"Ambre Solaire . . . ?" Soula extracts the bottle from

Kerrie's hands. "Is that strong enough?" she asks, slathering your shoulder blades in sun screener.

"He can't. He's a film producer." Act suave. "He says he has to live in the 'front line.' "

Kerrie flops onto the wheezing lilo she's just inflated. "You really want plutonium in your porridge?"

Soula sunbakes with a round corn pad on each pale nipple. "How married is he?"

"Sprogs," you confess. "But the marriage is dead. They're just going through the motions. He'll move in with me and we'll work together and . . ."

"Married men"—the air valve hisses asthmatically as Kerrie squirms into a new position—"have a history of *staying* married."

"Yeah," confirms Soula. Break the news to her that corn pads are to kill corns. Her nipples might fall off.

Your friends lecture you on the collective Stick Sister mythology. They list the hordes of Aussie girls who have had their hearts broken in the Northern hemisphere.

"It's the *country* they fall in love with here. The hedonism, the heat, the classlessness, our rapport with nature . . ."

Julia rummages in her bag then surrounds all four of you in a force field of insect repellent. You hope it will also ward off the busload of Japanese tourists pouring onto the beach. Sweltering in suits and ties, they cluster at the water's edge, the ladies' high heels embedded in the soggy sand. "The way we accept people as they are . . ."

"Bulk Nips," Debbie whispers commando-style. "Ten o'clock high." A couple with a camera approach to ask if they can take a photo of Julia's well-endowed mammaries. It is the second Japanese invasion of the Pacific, only this time they are armed with nine-calibre Kodaks. Her Speedos rolled down to her hips, Kerrie throws a bare arm round a startled Nippon. He scurries crablike back to his bus.

"The bloody brain-drain to London is over," Julia exclaims. You watch sunburn blotches develop with the speed of a Polaroid print along Kerrie's buttocks and peer dubiously over your sizzling shoulder. "Sydney is as cosmopolitan as anywhere else in the world," Julia insists. "We're just as sophisticated . . ."

"Fuck, I wish I spoke Frog. . . . Are you sure about the protection factor of this, Soula?" Kerrie scrutinises then reads aloud the small print, " 'Crème Après Soleil.' " What does *that* mean?"

It is decided that you are not going to England. Your Stick Sisters agree that Poms are sexually repressed—they always want you to wear suspenders and be spanked. They're allergic to baths and tight-arsed—they only shout if there's a shark.

By the time you all roll over, coat cream on knees, nipples, necks, and wriggle and rearrange the sand, the sun is disappearing behind a wad of thick grey cloud.

He writes in a love letter that he hopes and prays the planet's serendipity angels engineer a chance for you to be together again soon. Angels be buggered. You ring an airline.

Because one of the things he loves about you is your spontaneity, you decide to arrive unannounced and to throw away your emergency list of rellos twice, thrice removed, as well as the address of the maiden aunt of your hairdresser's lover's masseuse. Soon you'll be sipping Lapsang Souchong and dipping into discussions on Existentialism. Melvyn is profoundly, passionately, poetically in love with you. You are as certain of this as of the fact that England is a tea-bag–free zone.

Track him down. Hurl yourself at him in Harrods. He pulls back in horror. "Sorry . . . My damn classicism . . ." he mumbles, looking round nervously. "It holds me back . . ." You realise that Englishmen adore a little spontaneity—as long as they get a warning.

"Well, Ro, what do you, from a younger continent, make of Europe from this visit?" All you can make of it so far is that you only have another half hour in the room. He tells you that one of the great things about walking around London with you and going to galleries is that everything suddenly takes on a new aura. Lick the socket of his armpit. He giggles, squirms, then sighs. "Why am I, why are we Europeans, so gloomy, so . . . lugubrious?"

Tell him it is not a visit.

Your cups of room-service tea by the bed are as brown and cold as the Thames. "There are complications," he gulps. You realise that nobody speaks plain English in England. It's a surrogate-mother tongue. You need United Nations headphones to decipher the euphemisms. "Spot of trouble on the home front" decodes as career, kids, mortgage, and marriage to Octavia.

Register her name. Octavia. You just know she wears a bun and tweed skirts, does cryptic crosswords, moans in Latin, and can pull poetic quotes and the biographical details of Donne out of thin (is it really radioactive?) air.

Ask for suggestions about where you should live.

He looks panicked. "Have you ever noticed," he distracts you with kisses, "that the great lovers in European literature are always dying in each other's arms? Romeo and Juliet, Tristan and Isolde, Lancelot and Guinevere, Troilus and Cressida? The most beautiful love stories in this continent are always about loss. Loss in love," he stresses, "is a great European tradition."

Topping up the tea, you notice the string of a tea bag trailing forlornly from the pinched little mouth of the pot.

He takes you to a club called Groucho's. It is chock-a-block with producers and poets and playwrights and dons with multitudes of chins. They're all signing up each other for books and films of the book and videocassette novelisations of the radio musical. When they discover you are from

Or-strail-yar, it is as though they have collectively trodden in a dog turd.

"Your economy's keeling over what? Your country's been out to lunch for too long." You detect a trace of envy in the mangled vowels of his educated voice. Melvyn introduces him as a famous Shakespearean actor from the Lakelands. "Known in the colonies, no doubt, for its pencils," the Shakespearean actor chortles.

"Any lead in yours?" you ask sweetly. England brings out the worst in you. It makes you want to talk about pillow biters and pointing percy at the porcelain.

"Not another creative little person from the colonies? Surely we've taken in enough of you by now." Tell him you are working on an anti-British, all-lesbian review called "The Loneliness of the Long-Distance Punner on a Hot Tin Spoof." Melvyn's lips tighten as he tells everyone you have jet lag, then hisses in your ear that puns are the lowest form of wit.

He doesn't return your calls for three days. Go to Foyles bookshop. Look up the plots of Troilus and Cressida and Tristan and Isolde in Kobbé's *Complete Opera Book*. Stuck in some bleeding-heart plot, they invariably get stabbed and then can't stop singing. Vocal haemophiliacs.

It is a strange country. The intellectuals want to fuck Margaret Thatcher. And everybody else wants to work as Lady Di's hairdresser and sell their memoirs. On freezing cold days they sunbathe on deckchairs in Hyde Park, nipples rising off their anaemic chests like little pink ice blocks.

Ensconced in your bed-sit (thus named because there is only one place to sit—on the bed), it's like making love in a knapsack. "Constrictus Claustrophobis" is your big effort at moaning in Latin. You ask him how much longer he's going to go through the motions?

"The expatriot's anguish. Oh, how brave you are, Ro."

He dresses quickly, each buttonhole stitching him up tighter, his morals now as kempt as his silk cravat. "The experience of exile is rather cubist, don't you think?" Pat his black leather elbow patches as though they're the cold noses of a couple of stray dogs. "You live in an impacted space, really. The presence of the country you're living in and the memories of home. Tragic." He steeplechases over the bed and is off on the home stretch.

When you don't hear from him for a week, you write a list of every Pommy joke you know . . . Where do Poms hide their money? Under the soap.

After you threaten to drink a death draught, he takes you to the Royal premiere of his new film. Octavia is attending a conference in Brussels on the "Revival of Obsolete Dialects." Melvyn suggests you wear your best frock. A brace of Royals are doing the rounds. You promise to raise your Corgi Consciousness and to not split any of your infinitives.

"G'day," you greet Lady Di. It is amazing how even the lefties and radicals go limp at the thought of meeting a Royal. London is a peerage-hungry principality. Her gravity-defying hairstyle is a miracle of technology. Wonder if her brains are blow-waved too. You inquire as to Her Highness's favourite television show.

"Dynasty," she replies, eyeing off your leather mini skirt. Everyone else is wearing long chiffon. You finally learn the difference between a frock and a dress. You wear a dress. A frock wears you. Why does she like *Dynasty?* "Oh," she says, "I enjoy the escapism."

It strikes you that for Lady Di, *Dynasty* would be a documentary. What she should be watching is a soapie about the Brixton riots. "I don't like the women in *Dynasty* much," you confess. "They're not real. None of those ladies ever get blackheads or period cramps." There is a sudden intake of breath around you, like a giant asthma attack. Perhaps blue bloods don't get periods? Melvyn's face drains of all expression. You fidget and twitch, then lurch onto a new subject. "There's something I've always wanted to ask you . . ." Faces freeze as her minders wait for you to ask about the duration of her orgasms, the location of her G-spot, and whether or not she likes the odd bit of bondage covered in custard. "Have you mastered the art of yawning with your mouth closed?" She is whisked away from your vicinity and Melvyn steers you from the room by the elbow. As you leave, you overhear Princess Di telling some cricketing star you've seen on the back of a porridge pack that what she enjoys most about cricket is the escapism.

Melvyn's house is huge and full of panelled, port-stained studies and four-posters. You drink too much then drop your champagne flute. "Don't worry." Melvyn's smile is one of the particularly stiff variety, adopted by a host when a drunken guest drops one of his champagne glasses. "The eighteenth century was very long. I'm sure they made many more of them."

Draped on the chaise longue, you announce that if you lived together, you could stay in bed for a month. You tell him the aim would be to kiss the remotest creases of his human milk-bottle body.

He informs you casually that Octavia's father is an Earl. Or is it a Knight? Something related to the personage on the postage stamp, anyway. "Divorce lacks that certain noblesse oblige," he explains.

Reply that you thought breeding was something they did with dogs.

"Your country's hang-ups—your isolation and ex-colonial unease—are so much healthier than ours," Melvyn pontificates, strapping you into high heels and corset. As he brandishes a riding crop, remind yourself that the English are more prone to eccentricity than any other nation.

He is busy. On location. So you eat afternoon tea in the Savoy, as many cream cakes as possible for four pounds. Oh well, you tell yourself, you only live twice. Once now, and once after the triple-bypass heart surgery. The emergency list of maiden aunts and rellos now looks like a good idea. Kerrie and Debbie send you a chop, express airmail. You become unbearably homesick, catch a cold, and jam your stockinged, icicled toes up the hot-air hand dryer in the ladies' loo at Harrods to thaw out.

Thatcher is like a cold England can't shake off. Kinnock runs round with the Kleenex, mopping up, but it has already penetrated deep into the country's chest. Up close, the punks pictured on the postcards smell of soap and Blue Clinic shampoo. Your cold turns into the twenty-four-hour flu. Your penicillin capsules run out at twenty-three hours. Your daily highlight is to watch the passing parade of the Changing of the Guard, England's version of Disneyland. You begin to think that perhaps Melvyn is right; against the greyness and angst of a wintry London, Australia shimmers with possibilities.

"Australia is the flavour of the month in England," you enthuse on postcards back to your pals. And you sit with fellow expatriates telling each other how famous Paul Hogan and Peter Carey and Clive James are and how fashionable it is for Australians to be sitting round in London, talking about how fashionable it is to be Australians sitting round in London.

Melvyn must be right when he emphasises to you the importance of Australia on the world map. It is the place of the future. The place for the brave. The last chance of the republican dream. You believe him now when he says he'll be down under often.

You're in a travel agency, booking a return flight, and decide to stop off in Hawaii, the Cocktail Capital of the

World. Browsing through the accommodation brochure, you see an article about Captain Cook. "The greatest discovery Captain Cook ever made was the Hawaiian Islands." Raising one eyebrow, you read on. "The Queen of England sent him to sea to discover the Great Southern Unknown land, which he never discovered." "Cooee!" you call out to nobody in particular, in the middle of Piccadilly Circus. "We are there!"

Cover him in kisses. Promise that your Dag Days are over. No longer will you wear blue with black or sprout maverick patches of armpit stubble. You promise not to poke fun at his paunch in public—no more jokes about a verandah over the toy shop.

Since your arrival in England, Melvyn's emotional terrain has bristled with barbed wire. You pole-vault over it to tell him how much you love and need and adore him. But he frog-marches you back onto firmer ground—safer topics, like terrorism and the storing of nuclear waste.

"You English men are so different in your own warren compared with how you appear in my neck of the wood." The grey pavement is lumpy with cobblestones, it feels like you're walking on what they served you up for breakfast. "You come to my country and reinvent yourselves."

"Maybe we are reinvented? But we do all fall to dreams of love in Australia. Is it the light? It *must* be the light that makes the English male libido never want to wear underpants again!"

Your tan has faded. Your freckled skin looks like a game of join-the-dots. You worry that if you joined them all up you'd turn out to be a donkey . . .

"Remember, you are a light in my life," he says, leaving for location in Canada. "Blossom, I want you to feel secure in the fact that for me there will only ever be you . . . and Octavia."

* * *

"Well . . ." Julia Frisbees her sun hat onto your head, "what happened?"

Feel yourself dissolving in the midday sun. "Australia only exists so that England has something it can feel superior to . . . oops." Remember he's an Oxford graduate. "As a place to which England can feel superior."

"But I thought he loved this country?" Kerrie lies rigid in a G-string, eyes searching neurotically for stray pubes. "I thought he was a direct descendant of Captain Cook for God's sake?"

Talk posh. Polish your vowels. Try not to cry. "So?" you retort. "No woman is a continent."

"God," Julia groans, "why do women *always* end up the victims?"

When Narelle got dumped by her English fiancé, she sued unsuccessfully for breach of promise. Gail had a nervous breakdown in Brighton, became celibate, went through est, and is now in full-time therapy and a part-time job at the London branch of the Australia Council. Remember *your* last day in London. You wept into your copy of Shakespearean love sonnets, then scaled his study desk, took down the curtain rail, removed the stoppers on each end, and filled the hollow railing with raw prawns. Your noblesse just refused to oblige.

You read in the papers that England is having an unexpected heat wave. Imagine Melvyn tearing up floorboards and ripping off wallpaper, searching for the source of the odour.

Pretty off, you know. Well, what do you expect? After all, you're just a girl from the colonies.

Girls' Night Out

The Shower Tea

All your friends are getting married. Every Saturday you bake an obligatory plate of lamingtons, gift wrap a Tupperware beetroot strainer, and mooch off to a suburban lounge room for a shower tea. This week it's Kylie's. Mums, distant cousins, neighbours, and school mates circumnavigate the cakes, cackling and clucking. "You'll be next, Jo." You squirm under their scrutiny. "Isn't it time you settled down and had some kiddies?"

As the bride-to-be is buried alive beneath a mound of teatowels, placemats, spice jars, oven mitts, dish racks, teapots, and tablecloths, guests strain anxiously to see who has given the most expensive prezzie. Girlfriends eye your beetroot strainer with disdain. It is clear you like Kylie $5.68 cents less than everyone else does. Some of the presents look pretty familiar. That elephant tusk bookend and ceramic animal miniature have done the 21st *and* shower tea rounds at *least* twice.

As you pass the parcel, musical chair, and pin the tail on the donkey, you decide you'd rather endure walking on hot coals, bound feet, or a bone through the nose than suffer the suburban matrimonial ritual. It will never be time to settle down and have some kiddies. Never, ever, ever.

The Engagement Party

At engagement parties you eat meat pies and pav. High heels embedded in the soggy paspalum, you stand in the shivering cluster round the punch. Dads dole out beer from two garbage cans brimming with melting ice. Boys scrum boisterously for their tinnies. Girls compare rings, scrutinising your hand. "Has he asked ya yet?"

Assure yourself that your friends are only getting married because it makes it easier to get deposits for the block of land at Menai. They should make their wedding vows in Real Estate Agencies. To have and to sharehold. To honour and repay. Till repayments do us part.

The Girls' Night Out

Meet your friends at Choy's Chinese BYO for a Girls' Night Out. You are best friends. Since school you've squeezed each other's blackheads. Compared cellulite. Told each other you look thin. Lied about bad root perms. Advised each other to tint brown bits black and black bits blond and where to put the pink and orange streaks through the middle to make it look more *natural*. Straggled behind in public to check for period spotting. Compared contraceptive techniques. And reassured each other that your men were either total sleaze schmuckos or hot spunk rats. None of you has an eighteen-carat fiancé.

Order exotic cocktails with umbrellas sticking out the top. As the night wears on, it becomes harder and harder to memorise orders. "Two Kahlúas, one Fluffy Duck, three Harvey Wall Bangers, two Leg Openers . . . um." Tell your friends that if you ever *do* get married, your man will have the shower tea, and you'll have the bucks' party. Because he likes cooking. And you like men.

"How *is* your boyfriend?" Kerrie asks, patting her new root perm. (She maintains the salon moved for her.) "Are you still seeing that sax player from INXS? God Jo, you're anorexic." She thrusts the peanut bowl at you. "The last time I saw anything that thin there was toothpaste in it." They all laugh. Four or five years younger than the rest, you try to ignore their smiles dripping with kind condescension. A case of smother-love.

"Oh, he's excellent," you report neutrally. "How's Russell?"

"Oh! Fab. He's leaving his wife any minute now and we're moving into his apartment at Kirribilli." Kerrie is twenty-three, gets her eyebrows styled, works in television, and has tried every diet from the Grapefruit to the Beverly Hills to the High-Sexuality Low-Cal Carbohydrates Only. "Imagine it, girls. A His and Her Harbour View!"

Ro rolls her eyes. Having tried hippy-tripping, Punk, psychoanalysis, est, merchant banking, Zen, Englishmen, and rebirthing, she is now, at twenty-three, into radical celibacy.

Julia, smelling of chlorine and garlic, announces that her new love might drop by later. Julia wears no makeup, always meets her journalistic deadlines, girl-cotts products from South Africa, and, at twenty-four and a half, is the Grown Up amongst you.

You all turn on her, horrified. "Jules. We agreed. It's a *Girls'* Night Out!"

"It *is* a girl."

Debbie pants up the stairs, full of apologies, only in time for the prawn cutlets. Debbie is blond and bronzed and dating an A grade political journo on the *Fin Review*. It's true love. She'd drink the water out of his Jacuzzi. "I've been sitting outside in his car for *heaps*. Didn't want him to know I couldn't find the friggin' door handle." Look at her, puzzled. "Well! . . . Then he'd sus it was my first time in a Ferrari."

The rest of you swap appalled glances. Kerrie orders Debbie a side order of brains. "You need all the help you can get, Deb."

Soula announces that Garry is finally leaving his wife and moving in with her. Kerrie bristles. "God, it must be great having such little tits, Sue. Clothes must hang so well." Soula adjusts her Sportsgirl cotton top and slumps in the corner like a brown paper parcel. No one else pays any attention. Kerrie is the Navratilova of the backhanded compliment.

During the pub crawl round the Rocks, Debbie speculates on the potential lesbians in your touch-footy team. "You can tell by their short nails. Heaps better for lovemaking apparently," she giggles. Fingers curl self-consciously round glasses of Bacardi and Coke. Eyes fidget. Debbie is perplexed by the stern silence. "Look, I hate to spread gossip, but, well, what else can I *do* with it?"

"I bet that's not *all* you're spreading." Kerrie glares as she stubs out her cigarette.

You deliver diversionary school reminiscences. The day Julia set fire to the science block. The time they hid the boys' bags on the roof of the auditorium. The dance night when Kerrie laid the student teacher on the oval. Ro reports that she's seen Tracey, the infamous footy freak. "Single mother. Two kids."

There is a collective sigh of derision. Julia proposes a

toast. May you never be trapped into a career of caressing.

"God, we used to look up to her heaps, remember?" Deb sighs. "She was so much older than us. A real rager. And so spunky."

"Yeah," says Kerrie. "And now she's nothing more than a sperm spittoon."

Vow never to settle down and have kiddies. Never, ever, ever.

The Strip

Queue with the Tennis Club Christmas parties and Hens' Nights celebrants at Jamison Street. Peer at the poster advertising the male stripper. "Our husbands think we're playing *bingo*," confesses Charlene from the Mortdale Mothers' Club. High heels paw the club carpet. "My Harry reckons it's disgustin' to look at other people's *things*." Undeterred, you and your friends stampede through the entrance.

In leather jock strap and studded dog collar, Flesh Gordon bounds onstage. Leg cocking and gyrating, he is like a poodle let off the leash. "Oh God," shrieks Soula, her terminals rising. "He's a dead ringer for our plumber. That guy from Macquarie Fields!!"

"He's only about *that* big," hisses a disappointed Debbie, extending her pinky in demonstration.

Waiting at the bar, you feel bored by the surrounding conversation. Conceptual infrastructures. Designer lettuce. Short-term interest rates. Wish you could continue the philosophical discussion begun on Saturday at the local cricket match. After the game a seven-year-old girl had confided that there were two Gods. "God in and god out," she'd informed your kneecap matter-of-factly. Laugh. Wonder if you could just have the kids, without settling down. Feel anxious. *Pre-*natal, pre-*conceptual* depression. Talk about getting in before the rush. On the way back to the table, you pass Flesh Gordon prowling through the audience.

"But Julia, what about the biological urge?"

Julia squirms. "I'm a *career* woman. I don't have a biological urge to spend all my spare time stopping some miniature delinquent from dropping the guinea pig down the dunny."

"You want them, don't you, Debbie? *You* love kids."

"Get real! I'm broke. The friggin' tooth fairy probably takes bankcard by now."

"Come on. Don't you want to be pregnant one day, Ro? You like to try everything."

"Yeah, but I'm not a space cadet." She tucks a two-dollar tip down the jocks of the moustachioed waiter. "I mean, what if it grew up into a car salesman?"

A communal gasp of horror.

"Or *worse,*" Julia cringes into her whiskey. "A National party supporter!!!"

"Yeah, who cares about an embryo's *sex?*" Kerrie stands up. She has developed a severe starboard list. "What I want is an ultrasound which detects his or her future profession. Plus some other vital info. Like . . . will it clean up its room? Is it ever going to vote for Joh Bjelke Peterson?" Watch her tack towards the toilets. "Anyone wanna come blow a number?"

"I dunno," you waver, "maybe motherhood really does fulfill you? You know. As a woman."

The male stripper rubs catlike against you, confiscates your glasses, and deposits them down his leather pouch. You're blindfolded and told to retrieve them with your teeth. The "Use By" date on the disco tune has definitely expired. You suddenly feel ancient. Mouldy. Geriatric. In the dark, your secret white spencer glows fluorescent through your glam silk top. Feeling about as aroused as you do at the dentist, you descend into the subterranean claustrophobia of his jock strap.

"That's s'posed to make you feel *all woman* too," Julia rebukes triumphantly.

"And what about the bloody *pain?"* Ro protests, her nails jammed between her teeth. "I need a Mogadon to go to the dentist. Just for fluoride."

"Apparently the first shit afterwards is heaps worse than the actual childbirth!" Debbie grimaces in mock agony as she reapplies lippy.

"I was 'support person,'" Julia lectures, wolfing nuts, "for a friend of mine from the Women's Film Co-op. When the doctor was sewing her up after the episiotomy, she told him to just keep on sewing." The collective crossing of legs is audible. "She didn't want anything going *in,* or coming *out* of there ever again."

"Shit," commiserates Kerrie, back from the toilets, her bloodshot eyes widening, "and those women are tough. I mean they roll their own tampons."

"Not only that, but for the rest of your life, you've got to do," Julia lowers her voice conspiratorially, *'pelvic floor exercises."* Your ears wag with horrified fascination as Julia goes into a graphic description of how the vaginal muscles must be contracted into a vicelike grip, then relaxed, one hundred times, morning and night and at boring moments. This gives a whole new dimension to loo queues and bus stops. While you wait in line at the Ladies', flickering away internally like a fluorescent light on the blink, you search the other female faces, trying to discern who else is giving a quick jog to her G zone. No, tell yourself, no settling down and kiddies. Never, ever, ever.

Soula follows you to the toilets. "Maybe you're right, Jo," she hazards, "maybe we'll just all end up lonely . . ." Steel yourself. Tell her yes, that it's hard not to pity all those

197

childless couples floating on Sydney Harbour on Sundays, anaesthetising their sadness with Dom Perignon and pâté.

She talks to you from the cubicle next door. "I mean, maybe we'll miss out on heaps of joy and stuff." Yes, just think of all the walkathons you won't have to sponsor. Monopoly games you won't have to play. The Mayfairs and Park Lanes you won't be beaten to. No, tell her firmly. Never, ever, ever . . . Swagger back to the table. Tell your friends that the cognoscenti might be big on Leboyer, but you've decided to be an advocate of unnatural childbirth. The only way you can be talked into parenthood is if you can have daily epidurals from the moment of conception till the child reaches twenty. They back-pat approvingly and pledge never to settle down and have kiddies. Never, ever, ever.

The music crescendoes. Flesh Gordon's buttock cheeks quiver like custard. He pulls the final string. Exposure with composure. Watch his genitalia execute a series of gymnastic feats. It whirls lasso-like, then stretches and contracts like a piece of hat elastic. A pelvic push-up or two, and it's all over. The audience gaze at each other. "Gord," says a mum from the Cabramatta Tennis Club, "it beats bingo."

Stripping Off to Emotional Undies

Buy a supply of CCs, chips, Norgen-Vaaz ice cream, beer, and McDonald's burgers. Scale the gates of the Botanical Gardens. Do handstands, cartwheels, and Lady Di impersonations. Count your lovers, memories lapsing at double digits. Compare the size of mens' cocks and laugh hysterically at stupid jokes explaining the rationale for the creation of man. Dildos can't put out the garbage . . .

Sprawl under the sliver of moon. It sits in the corner of

the sky like a toenail clipping. You decide that, what with Julia's big breasts hurting when she runs, period cramps, and childbirth, God is definitely a bloke. No. No settling down and having kiddies. Never, ever, ever. Mouche wouldn't go sprogging. Since Sushi days, she'd worked for the PLO, the IRA, and now back home she'd joined a nunnery—another form of terrorism and definitely no kids . . .

Make a groggy reconnaissance of your body. Your tongue feels furry. The *Down* syndrome, you quip. Hang on . . . That's *not* funny. Sober up. Mongoloid Fever suddenly sets in. Think to yourself that as the years blink by on the biological digital clock, the chances of having a handicapped child increase. Your snooze alarm suddenly goes off.

"Jo, you're *nineteen,*" Julia wearily admonishes. "No need to get Mongoloid Fever just yet."

Lights blink a mysterious Morse code on the water. Remorse code for you. Mentally pack your diaphragm permanently in cornflour. "Maybe we could all just have *one?*"

"Impossible." Julia crushes your proposal. "What if it's Oedipal?" Tell her you'll have two. "What if they fight?" Tell her three. "Oh yes, then a fourth to avoid the Third-Child Syndrome."

"But last children," Ro slurs drunkenly, "are spoilt rotten. Which means having a sixth, seventh, eighth . . ."

"Besides," Kerrie articulates slowly, as though you're lip-reading, "you'll bore your friends to death. Nothing double glazes my brain faster than all that talk about crèche waiting lists and . . . and early signs of genius."

Julia pontificates about statistics proving that the twenties are the most exciting and stimulating time of a woman's life. "We're in our prime, girls!!" she shouts with drunken fervour.

Vomit up your burger and beer.

They put your momentary aberration down to PMD:

Post McDonald's Depression. "Why would we want to settle down and have kiddies when we're all so successful, happy, fulfilled!?"

You sit forlornly on the damp grass and stare at the stars. "What's up?" Kerrie interrogates. "Did you get out of the wrong side of somebody's bed this morning?"

Confess that INXS does *not* have a sax player.

Soula sobs that in the staff room Garry acts as though he's never laid eyes on her. "Let alone laid you," Kerrie adds.

Soula comes clean that she has decided to marry her father's friend's son, Spiro, a real Dapto dog from the Old Country.

"Fuck it," Kerrie explodes into a volley of sneezes. The heater for her water bed has broken down. For a week she's been forced to go to bed wearing skivvy, gloves, and balaclava. "Russell is moving to L.A. with his wife and family. Let's just say there turned out to be a draught in his 'open' marriage."

Julia is by now well lubricated and full of remorse. She divulges that she's a ball-breaker. She's the reason Billy's back inside.

Debbie kicks off her shoes. "My Intellectual never even turned up." She admits to making up the lunches on harbour launches and the literary discussions at Berowra Waters. "He bites pillows," she whimpers. Tears leave a black trail through her blusher into the corners of her mouth.

Ro extricates herself from her lotus position. She whines that she gave up sex for aerobics, est, and swimming and is now more healthy, enlightened, and chlorinatedly bored than ever.

You all dive into an Olympic pool of self-pity. Wallow. Polish off the packet of CCs between you. "Oh well," you tell the others, "at least we know now what to do in those boring moments. Flex those vaginal muscles! Eighty-nine, ninety, ninety-one, ninety-two . . .'"

The Brekky

Laugh. Link arms. Kerrie says she has a bad case of the Zacclies. "When your mouth tastes zacclie like your arsehole." High heels in hand, walk by the Art Galley, down past the Woolloomooloo shop windows full of Santa Clauses in swimming costumes, up by the neon Coca-Cola sign blinking neurotically. Watch the dawn from the top of the Cross, sucking on the last of the tinnies. Buoyed up with camaraderie, you drink to "success." Inoculated with ambition, you make a pact. Yours is a burping-and-booty-free zone. Drink a toast to careers, not crèches. To board rooms, not babies' bottoms.

"Never will our vocabulary be limited to 'Elbows off the table; Don't pull a face, the wind might change,'" Ro exclaims.

You agree. No, no, never will you knit anything other than your eyebrows. Never, ever, ever.

Ooze with the confidence of being young, strong women in a young, strong country. Be thankful for having all the benefits of feminism but none of the battle scars. Slap each other on the back for being lucky enough to live in the Age of Options.

It's breakfast at the Bourbon and Beef Steak, yawning into cups of black coffee. You feel flat. The tide's gone out in your tummy. Maybe Soula's right. Maybe you will end up selfish and lonely, living in a vacuum. So much for the Age of Options. The only thing you've decided is that you can't decide. It's a passing nostalgia for the good old-fashioned, uncomplicated days . . . when you just got up the duff without doing it on purpose! Brood over the attractions of breeding: a cleavage, kids. Not only are they great philosophisers, but they never drop round at midnight to whinge about their de facto troubles, threaten to sue or take est courses.

Sitting round the table, you're serious, eighties sophisticates. The waiter hovers. Hashbrowns, croissants, ham-and-tomato omelettes. "That's what's so good about our generation," Julia lectures, menu tucked neatly underneath her teapot. "We're decisive. No fainthearted, gutless vacillation for us!"

"How would you like your eggs?"

Rationalise to yourself that car salesmen are not genetic, but created by their environment. Besides, it really does depend on the type of car. Secondhand panel vans? No way. But imported Porsches?

"Lady?"

Shrug. Look sheepish. Tell him "fertilised."

Kerrie chokes, spluttering orange juice all over Soula, who begins frantic frock-mopping. Debbie's chortle starts a chain reaction. Kerrie's cackle is contagious. Ro is now delirious. Julia's stern lips start to crease. The laughter subsides to a wheeze. "What's so funny?" Soula asks. This sets you all off again. You're laughing at each other's laughs, pointing fingers, clutching abdomens, choking, convulsed, mouths wide open, holding each other up, dizzy with delight, laughing and laughing, thrilled and aghast at your own hypocrisy.